Contents

True Friends

Robin Jones Gunn

PUBLISHING

Colorado Springs, Colorado

TRUE FRIENDS

Copyright © 1993 by Robin Jones Gunn

Library of Congress Cataloging-in-Publication Data
Gunn, Robin Jones, 1955-
  True friends / Robin Jones Gunn.
      p.   cm—(The Christy Miller series)
      Summary: New twists and turns abound in sixteen-year-old Christy Miller's
life as she finds herself on a ski slope inthe arms of a handsome ski instructor and
shares more madcap adventures with best friend Katie.
      ISBN 1-56179-131-8
      [1. Friendship—fiction. 2. Skis and skiing—fiction.] I. Title. II. Series:
Gunn, Robin Jones, 1955-
Christy Miller Series.
PZ7.G972Tr   1993
[Fic]—dc20   93-19978
                                                                    CIP
                                                                    AC

Published by Focus on the Family, Colorado Springs, Colorado 80995.

Distributed in the U.S.A. and Canada by Word Books, Dallas, Texas.

Scripture is from the Revised Standard Version, Copyright 1946 by Division of
Christian Education of the National Council of the Churches of Christ in the
United States of America. Second Edition, Copyright © 1971 by Division of
Christian Education of the National Council of Churches of Christ in the United
States of America.

Chapter 14:
From *The House at Pooh Corner*, A.A. Milne. Copyright © 1928, E. P. Dutton.
Renewed copyright © 1956 by A. A. Milne. Used by permission of Dutton
Childrens Books, a division of Penguin Books U.S.A., Inc.

Edited by Janet Kobobel
Cover illustration by David R. Darrow

Printed in the United States of America
94 95 96 97 98 99/ 15 14 13 12 11 10 9 8 7 6 5

In memory of my mother-in-law,
Katherine Beckman Gunn.
You were and always will be my True Friend.

Chapter 1

A Lightning Bolt From Heaven

Over the years lots of people have given their opinions on friendship. I would like this class to work off of the handout I've given you and write a three-page essay. Begin with the phrase, 'A true friend is . . . .' You may use the rest of the class time to work on it. Any questions?"

Sixteen-year-old Christy Miller glanced across her English class and noticed her friend Katie had her hand up.

"Is it okay if we use some of the quotes from the list?" Katie asked, her red hair swishing as she tilted her head.

"Of course you may. Now, no talking. This is project time."

Christy adjusted her long legs under the desk and studied the handout. The page was full of quotes from people like Constantine and Aristotle. She smiled when she read what Charles Dickens had to say about friends: "Friendship? Yes, please."

Taking out a fresh sheet of paper, she wrote at the top of the page, "A true friend is . . ."

Only one word came to mind: *Todd.*

That was not the word she was looking for. Christy pushed the thought aside and scolded herself.

Come on, you have lots of friends. What are you doing thinking of Todd? He's not even a part of your life anymore. Think, think, think. What is a true friend?

She began to write. "A true friend is someone who sticks up for you and . . ." *Todd,* her mind said again. ". . . and they always look for the best in you. A true friend likes you even when you don't like yourself very much."

Then, without meaning to, she wrote, "My true friend is Todd Spencer."

There. She finally admitted it to herself.

By writing it down, it was as if she had admitted to the world that Todd was her true friend.

How did Todd say it almost a year ago when he placed the engraved "forever" ID bracelet on her wrist? "Here's my friendship. I promise it to you. It's yours forever."

Christy thought of how Todd had backed up that statement about two months ago. It was early morning on a deserted beach. The night before, without really wanting to, Christy had agreed to go steady with Rick Doyle. There she was, in the early morning California fog, trying to explain it to Todd.

Christy had tried to give back the bracelet, but Todd

wouldn't take it.

"No matter what happens," he had said, "we're going to be friends forever."

Then he announced he was going to Hawaii to try out for the world-tour surfing team. She hadn't heard from him since.

Christy drew a tiny heart in the corner of her paper and let memories of Todd fill her mind. Each memory prompted a little doodle. Soon the margins danced with sketches of a tandem bike, a picnic basket with sea gulls circling over it, a bouquet of carnations, an old Volkswagen bus, and down the entire right side of her page, a waterfall crowned with a bridge across the top.

The shrill bell jolted her back to her Friday morning English class. Snapping shut her notebook, Christy grabbed her books and waited at the door for Katie.

"Did you get yours done?" Katie asked, her green eyes sparking like she had a secret.

"Not really," Christy said, pushing back her nutmeg brown bangs. They were growing out and driving her crazy. "Did you?"

"Almost," Katie said as they walked down the noisy hallway. "Who did you write about?"

"Well, I didn't come up with anything final yet," Christy said. "I guess I'm going to have to work on it this weekend."

"I wrote about the person I consider to be my truest friend in the whole world." Katie's eyes kept twinkling. "I want you to read it, but not until I'm finished."

A horrible feeling hit Christy. *Katie's acting as though she wrote about me! Like I'm her best friend. Katie has been a rock of a true friend to me, and I've taken her for granted.*

At lunch the girls met at their usual spot by the outdoor picnic tables. By then Christy had formed a plan. She wanted to do something that would let Katie know how much she appreciated her.

"Katie, I'm going to ask you something, and I want you to give me a straight answer."

"Okay, shoot."

"I want to know what you'd like to do together sometime. Just you and me."

"What do you mean?" Katie asked.

"What is something you'd like to do? Would you like to go shopping, or what? Name it."

"You're sounding like something's wrong, Christy. We do stuff together all the time. Why do we need to make special plans to do something together?"

Christy took a deep breath and stuffed the remainder of her sandwich back in her lunch bag. She hadn't figured it would be this complicated.

"Can I be honest with you?" Christy asked.

"No, I want you to lie to me," Katie said. Then, pushing Christy on the shoulder, she said, "I'm only kidding! What are you being so serious about? You're scaring me."

"Katie, you have been such a good friend to me. I feel as though I haven't been as good a friend back to you. You're the most gracious friend I've ever had."

"Gracious?" Katie repeated.

"Yeah, you know. Like last year when my aunt and uncle took me to Palm Springs. You didn't get to come because of the football game. You were so gracious about it—"

"But—" Katie started to interrupt.

Christy kept going, not letting Katie have a chance to disagree with her. "Then this summer when I went to Maui. You know I wanted to take you, but I had to take Paula with me because she was visiting that week. It was all set up by my aunt, and I didn't have any say about who went with me."

"I know, Christy. You don't have to explain."

"That's what I mean! You're always so supportive. You were gracious about Palm Springs and Maui. You were even gracious when Paula was a snip to you—"

"Christy," Katie finally cut in, "you're making it sound like I was being heroic. I wasn't. It killed me that I didn't get to go with you those times."

"But you didn't act like it. That's what I'm trying to say. You've always been supportive of me. Always."

"Well, almost always," Katie said. "If you will recall, I wasn't exactly supportive when you were dating Rick."

"Yes you were. You just had a strong opinion about Rick."

"I still have that opinion. I didn't need to say all those things to you about him, though," Katie said thoughtfully. "You handled the situation fine without my nasty comments."

"No," Christy disagreed, "I needed you to say those things. I needed to hear your opinion. And, as I've said before and will probably say a thousand times, you were right, Katie. Going out with Rick was a huge mistake."

"And as I've told you a thousand times," Katie said, "going out with Rick was not the problem. Going steady with him was. . . well, if you want my opinion, it was about the stupidest thing you've done in your entire life."

Christy laughed as Katie's honesty brushed over her. "Yeah, well, I guess some things I have to learn the hard way. You know, it still hurts when I think about him."

"Why? Because he was such a jerk, and he treated you like slime?"

"No, Rick didn't treat me badly; you know that."

"Yeah, right. He only stole the bracelet Todd gave you, hocked it to a jeweler, and is now making you buy it back with every paycheck until Thanksgiving. Silly me!" Katie slapped her forehead for emphasis. "I guess that's the way every girl dreams her boyfriend will treat her. I just haven't reached that level of maturity to understand such deep, caring, emotionally enriching relationships."

"All right, Katie," Christy said, throwing up her hands in surrender. "You're right! Okay? Rick was sort of a. . ."

"Grade-A, first-class, totally flaming jerk," Katie filled in for her.

"I guess you could put it that way," Christy gave in. "But he wasn't like that all the time. There's a tender side to him too. I'm not saying I want to go out with him again. It's just that I don't feel as though my relationship with Rick is resolved."

"You told him to get lost. What more needs to be resolved?" Katie asked.

"I can't explain it. I'm not sure I really know. I want him to understand why I broke up with him. One of these days I'd like to sit down with him and talk everything out."

Katie ventured slowly, "You mean the way you talked things over with Todd that morning on the beach? I mean, can you honestly say you now feel your relationship with Todd is over and resolved?"

Christy shook her head, feeling her hair tumble over her shoulders as she lowered her eyes. Uninvited tears brimmed her lower lids. "No," she said softly. "It's not over with Todd. I think about him all the time."

"So?" Katie perked up. "Why don't you write him? Send him a card. One of those cartoon ones. You told me your uncle gave you his address last week. What are you waiting for?"

"I don't know," Christy said, blinking back a tear. "A lightning bolt from heaven, I guess."

"Then here," Katie said, playfully bopping Christy on the head with a foil-wrapped Ding Dong. "Consider this your lightning bolt from heaven, and this is your message, 'Goeth thereforeth and writeth to Toddeth.' "

Christy laughed, her clear blue-green eyes making contact with Katie's. "Since you put it that way, okay, I will. I shalt goeth and buyeth a card todayeth."

Katie smiled her approval and said, "You know, an occasional bonk on the head with a Ding Dong seems to do you some good. Remind me to do that about every fifty thousand miles."

Not until Christy was sitting in her Spanish class after lunch did she realize Katie never had answered her original question. Christy still didn't know what Katie would like for the two of them to do together.

About the only time they had spent together during the summer was at church. Then school started, and Christy's job kept her busy every weekend.

When Christy started going out with Rick, Katie had talked about having the annual back-to-school slumber party at her house. Only Christy hadn't been able to find a free weekend night for the party, since she worked every Friday night and then had gone out with Rick on Saturdays after work. With Rick out of the picture, Christy thought maybe she could help Katie plan a slumber party with a bunch of girls like they had had last year.

Christy drove right from school to the mall, where her job at the pet store started at four. Her boss, Jon, greeted her with a big smile.

"Guess what?" Jon asked.

His long hair was pulled back in its usual ponytail, and he had on his typical jeans and T-shirt. Christy didn't notice anything different about Jon. It must be something about the shop.

She glanced around but didn't see anything that had changed. "I don't know. I give up. What?"

"I sold Walter this morning." Jon beamed.

Even the mention of Walter gave Christy the willies. She would never forget the night when the fifteen-foot python escaped from his cage and slithered out into the mall.

"You seem pretty happy about selling Walter," Christy said. "Beverly told me you'd had him forever. I didn't think you'd ever sell him."

"I did have him forever. Not because I was fond of him, but because nobody wanted to buy him. This morning some guy from Fallbrook came in and paid full price. Walter has a new home, and I couldn't be happier for him."

Jon picked up a clipboard from under the counter and said, "I've been meaning to ask you. Are you still happy with your hours, or do you want to change them so you can spend more time with your boyfriend?"

Christy felt her cheeks turn red. "Oh, no," she said quickly, "my hours are fine. I don't need to change them. Really."

Jon looked Christy in the eyes with the same scrutiny a doctor uses when checking a patient's throat. Then, as if he had found what he was looking for, he looked back at his clipboard and said, "I'm sorry."

Christy felt a little confused by his examination.

"You're sorry that I don't want to change my hours? I can change them or trade with somebody else, if you need me to."

"No, your hours are fine with me. As a matter of fact, they're great. I'm sorry you broke up with . . . what was his name?"

"Rick." The moment Christy said his name, she felt as though she had bitten into a wild, tangy raspberry.

"His name is Rick," she added, hoping to purge herself of the raspberry sensation. "We broke up about a week ago. But it's fine, really. We're just friends."

Jon looked her in the eye again. Then he flashed her a big grin, snapped the clip on top of the clipboard, stuck his pen behind his ear, and turned toward the back of the shop. "Well, I guess there comes a time when you have to say good-bye," he commented. "It's not always easy, but you've got to let the ol' snake go. Let somebody else have him for a while."

Christy was about to jump in and defend Rick, when Jon turned back to face her and said, "You know I'm talking about Walter, of course. That ol' snake, I mean."

"Right." Christy smiled back. "Walter. Of course. I knew that."

She slipped her purse under the counter and took her position behind the register.

Guys. Who needs them? Not me.

Christy began to straighten the counter top, ready to concentrate on work.

I'll show Jon and Katie and everyone else that I

don't need a guy in my life.

Taking a deep breath, she mumbled, "Now, if I can only convince myself, I'll be fine."

Chapter 2

The King of Returns

Excuse me," the customer in front of the register said to Christy. She had been working for more than an hour, but this was the first customer who had talked to her. All the rest had responded to her smile and "Have a nice day" with grunts and mumbles.

"Could you tell me when you're going to get more birdseed mix? You seem to be out; the bin is empty."

"I'm not sure, but let me ask the manager." Christy pushed the red button under the counter, and Jon came trotting up to the front.

As Christy explained to Jon about the birdseed, out of the corner of her eye she spotted Katie entering the shop.

"Our shipment comes in Monday," Jon told the customer. "Would you like us to call you when it arrives?"

"No, I would not like you to call me when it arrives," the man answered. "I would like it if you stocked your store well enough so you don't have to offer lame excuses and make me wait. What kind of a manager are you? You can't even keep your birdseed stocked."

With that, the man turned and marched out of the store.

"What's with that guy? Who does he think he is?" Christy asked.

"Oh, didn't I tell you? He's one of our best customers," Jon answered.

"Man, I'd hate to meet one of your worst customers!"

"You know what they say, 'The customer is always right.' Best thing to do is let it roll off you and keep going," Jon advised.

"But, Jon, he was rude to you, and he said a bunch of mean things."

"Weeds," Jon answered simply. "Maybe he was trying to toss a bunch of weed seeds in my garden. I don't need them."

"So what do you do?" Christy asked. "Ignore them?"

Jon looked at her as if she were young and had so much to learn. "If I ignore a bunch of weed seeds, they might take root and grow, right?"

"Right."

"And I'm certainly not going to fertilize and water those kinds of seeds for the fun of seeing what they look like when they sprout."

Christy nodded.

"So I pluck 'em up and throw 'em away," Jon said, using the appropriate hand motions. "Weeds belong in the compost pile, not in my garden."

Christy thought how unassuming Jon appeared. She

never would have guessed that her boss, the manager of a pet store, would come up with such insights into life.

Glancing at the clock behind the register, Jon said, "It's about time for your break. Why don't you take it now while your friend is here."

"Okay. And by the way, her name is Katie."

Pulling her purse out from under the counter and looping it over her shoulder, Christy called out, "It's okay, Katie. He's on to you. You don't have to act like a customer anymore."

Katie was standing behind a tall wire rack loaded with paperback books. She stuck her head around the rack. Only her green eyes showed above the book in her hand, titled *How to House-Train Your Rabbit in Only Twenty Days.*

"Nice to meet you, Katie," Jon called out as the girls scooted out of the shop.

"You too," Katie called over her shoulder.

Giggling, Christy asked, "Did you hear that man who came in right before you and wanted the bird-seed? Could you believe that guy?"

"I think he was having a bad day," Katie said, pulling Christy by the arm. "This way," she urged. "We're going to the gift shop to find a card for Todd."

"Boy, between you and Jon, nothing in my life is a secret!" Christy teased.

They entered the gift shop and steered down the greeting-card aisle.

"Let me pick out the card, okay?" Christy said.

"Of course," Katie agreed, stopping in front of a display of humorous cards. "I'm only here to offer my support."

"And your opinion," Christy added.

"And my opinion. But only if you want it," Katie said, as she lifted a card from the display and scanned it.

"Look!" Katie practically shouted, holding up the card. "This is it! This is perfect. The search has ended. I've found the perfect card. Read it."

"Katie," Christy scolded.

"I know, I know. You only wanted my opinion. Well, in my opinion, this is perfect. Didn't you tell me Todd has an orange surfboard?"

Christy snatched the card from Katie's eager, waving fist and looked it over. On the front was a drawing of a lone surfer on a bright orange board, riding the crest of a huge wave and shouting, "Surf's up!" All the cartoon surfers on the beach were grabbing their boards and scrambling over each other in a muddled attempt to join the surfer.

Christy opened the card. Inside it said, "So, what's up in your end of the world?"

"Well," Katie said eagerly, "for a guy who left civilization to surf all winter on Oahu's North Shore, is this the perfect card, or what? And can you believe it? It even has an orange surfboard! Now is that odd, or is that God?"

Christy was laughing by now. "All right, you've convinced me. This is the perfect card for Todd. Let's pay for it, and then I'll treat you to a frozen yogurt next door. Remind me to ask you something."

A few minutes later, they were both scooping chocolate yogurt from their small cups and heading back to the pet store.

"So, what did you want to ask me?" Katie said.

"You never answered me at lunch today about what you want to do together. I thought maybe we could organize that yearly slumber party. I know it's October already, but we could still pretend it's a back-to-school party," Christy said.

Katie shook her head. "I've tried at least three times to organize it, but it just isn't going to happen. I guess we've all grown up. Maybe high school juniors are too old for slumber parties."

She scooped another spoonful of yogurt. "You know, our first party was the year we started sixth grade. Most of those girls aren't interested anymore."

"Why not?"

"Some of them have moved. Most of them have boyfriends or they work. Nobody wanted to have one this year except me."

"And me," Christy added. "I admit I was too busy with Rick and my job and being on restriction and everything right when school started. But I really want to have a slumber party now. Even if it's just the two of us."

Katie brightened. "Do you really? When? Any night is fine with me."

"How about tomorrow night? Could we pull it together that fast?" Christy asked.

"Sure! I can make a few calls to some girls and pick up a few bags of chips, some TP, and M&M's. What time can you be there?"

"I get off work at six, so if my parents say it's okay, I'll come right from work," Christy suggested.

"Perfect! I'll go home and clear a space in the freezer. You know, all the usual pre-party preparations."

"Why do you need to clear a space in the freezer?" Christy asked.

"It's tradition to freeze someone's underwear. Whose did we do last year? We try not to get the same person two years in a row."

"I don't remember," Christy said. "But can we just say it was mine so they won't do it to me this year?"

Katie laughed, and Christy knew that Katie was happy and excited about the party. It made Christy feel glad they were going to do it. But it also made her feel bad that she had put Katie on hold so many times in the past.

"I'll order the pizza at six," Katie said, "so it'll be there when you arrive. This is going to be great!"

The next afternoon, while Christy was at work, Katie called with an update on the party plans. Christy was in the back of the store marking prices on cans of fish food, which made it convenient for her to keep working while she talked.

"I have my sleeping bag and everything in the car,"

Christy said. "My parents were super nice and said I could keep the car all night. I don't have to be home until after church tomorrow. The only thing is, they don't want me to drive tonight if we go out papering houses. I can only drive to your house and then to church in the morning."

"Sounds good," Katie said. "I've called about fifteen girls. So far only three can come, but you never know. Some of them might show up later."

"Sure," Christy said, trying to sound optimistic, "you never know who else might come. Who is definitely coming?"

"You, me, and Teri."

Christy's heart sank when she realized she and Katie were two of the three. Katie deserved better. She deserved a house full of adoring friends who appreciated her for the true friend she was.

"Teri's coming? Really? That's great!" Christy said, covering up her disappointment. She had tried out for cheerleader with Teri last spring and had been wanting a chance to get to know her better ever since.

"Teri's coming for part of it, but she probably can't spend the night. You know, her dad is a pastor. He doesn't like his kids staying out late on Saturday nights, because one time Teri's brother was up late and fell asleep in the front pew on Sunday morning. I guess he tumbled onto the floor or something and disrupted the whole service. Anyway, Teri said it's a family rule now that everyone has to be in bed by eleven on

Saturday night."

"Ouch!" Christy said.

"What happened?"

"I just was trying to open this box, and I smashed my thumb. Oh no!" Christy started to laugh. "Katie, you're not going to believe this."

"What?"

"Guess what's in the box?" Christy said.

"What?"

"Birdseed! It's a huge box of birdseed, but someone wrote 'fish food' on the side of it. Just think, we could've satisfied that birdseed man last night after all. I have to tell Jon. I'll see you around six-thirty. We'll have a great time tonight, you'll see."

Christy hung up the phone and went to find Jon. Her coworker Beverly was standing behind the register helping a young boy. He was counting out his pennies to see if he had enough to buy a plastic treasure chest for his aquarium.

"Is Jon around?" Christy asked her.

"He should be right back. He went to return a shirt," Beverly explained, her silver bracelets clinking on the counter as she helped to count out the pennies.

"Didn't he return a shirt last week?" Christy asked.

"I think that was a pair of pants. Haven't you noticed how Jon shops? He buys stuff first and then decides if he likes it. He's the king of returns. All the department stores here at the mall have his credit card numbers memorized from seeing them so often. First when he buys the stuff, and then when he returns it."

Beverly turned to the boy and said, "Looks like you need twenty-seven cents more."

The little boy's face fell. "That's all I have."

"Here," Christy said, reaching for her purse, "I'm sure I have a quarter and a couple of pennies. Go ahead and ring it up, Beverly."

"Thanks," the boy said, shooting Christy a big smile. "And if I change my mind, can I return it?"

Beverly and Christy both laughed, and Beverly said, "If you do, make sure you ask for Jon. He's the king of returns around here."

Just then Jon walked in with a bag in each hand.

"I thought you were going to return something," Beverly teased.

"I did. Now I'm trying to decide what to get my sister for her birthday."

He held up the bag in his right hand and said, "It's either a vase or," holding up the bag in his left hand, "perfume."

Looking to Beverly and Christy for advice, he said, "Which do you think would be best?"

At the same moment, Christy answered "Perfume" and Beverly said "The vase."

"You two are a lot of help," Jon said. Then, heading toward the back of the shop, he added, "Oh well, I don't have to mail it until next Friday. I should be able to decide by then. I'll just take the other one back."

"What did I tell you?" Beverly said, swishing her

long braid back to where it belonged, trailing down her back. "The king of returns."

Right then Christy caught a glimpse of a guy in the mall. He looked an awful lot like Rick.

Making her way over to the front window, she pretended to work on the dog cage's latch while she scanned the mall for Rick. But she didn't see him anywhere.

Maybe I have my own king of returns, returning to my life. Rick said he wouldn't be back from college until Thanksgiving, but I wouldn't put it past him to secretly check up on me.

Letting go of the latch on the dog cage, she realized her hands were shaking. *What's wrong with me? I shouldn't feel this way about seeing Rick. We live in the same town, so we're bound to run into each other. I have no regrets and nothing to hide.*

Christy clenched her fist. Now she felt mad. Rick had had this strange power over her ever since she first met him, more than a year ago. As a matter of fact, it had been the night of Katie's slumber party. The girls had papered his house, and he had chased Christy down the street. For a whole year he had pursued her. She finally dated him, and then she broke up with him. But obviously thinking about him still caused her stomach to flip-flop.

Why am I like this? Is this normal? I hate this feeling. I never know when it's going to strike, and it's so hard to make it go away.

"Christy," Jon called from the back, "what's with this box of birdseed?"

Her feelings about Rick disappeared quickly. As Christy joined Jon in the back, everything switched from heart-pounding to normal in a matter of minutes.

But that evening, after work, the sweaty-palm feeling hit again.

Chapter 3

Pass the M&M's

"I'd like to make a payment on a bracelet you're holding for me," Christy said to the salesclerk at the jewelry store.

She stopped in every Saturday after work to pay off Todd's bracelet, which Rick had used as a down payment for a bracelet he had bought her. "It's under Miller. Christy Miller."

"Just a moment," the tall, blond woman replied. She made her way to the back of the store, where she spoke to the manager in hushed tones.

The manager looked up, and recognizing Christy, picked up a box and came out to the counter.

"Christy Miller," the older man said with a toothy smile. "How are you?"

"Fine, thanks. I just came in to make my weekly payment." She couldn't figure out why he was being so friendly and grinning at her that way.

"No need," he said, holding out the box. "It's all yours. Paid in full."

"I-I-I don't understand," Christy stammered. "I still have five more payments."

"Nope," the man said, placing the long, slim box in her hand. "A certain party, who wishes to remain anonymous, has paid it off. You can take it with you today."

"Who? What certain party?"

"Sorry. Can't tell you. He wishes to remain anonymous."

"He?" Christy whispered to herself. *Not Rick. Rick would never have done this. Or would he? He knew how upset I was that he stole it. Is it at all possible Rick returned the silver bracelet he gave me to get my gold one back?*

"Go ahead," the man said. "Put it on. I cleaned it for you this afternoon. No charge. It's a beautiful bracelet."

Christy felt as though this was almost a sacred moment. It certainly wasn't one she wanted to share with the jewelry store manager.

"Thank you very much," she said, tucking the unopened box into her purse. "I really appreciate it. Thank you." She backed up and quickly made her exit so she wouldn't feel forced to open the box in front of him.

She hurried back to the pet store, where she planned to slip out the back door and into the parking lot. Jon was sitting at the card table in the back room, going through the day's mail.

"Good night," she called out as she breezed past him. "See you next week."

"Glad to have your bracelet back?" Jon asked, without appearing to look up from his letters.

Christy stopped and spun around, astounded. "How did you know?"

Then it struck her that Jon knew she was making payments because the jewelry store manager had called him to check on her credit.

"You didn't pay for this, did you? Because if you did, well, I was paying for it, and I'll pay you back."

Jon looked at her as if he didn't understand a word she was saying.

"You can take it out of my paycheck, really. Every week until it's paid off." Christy caught her breath. "I appreciate it, but you didn't have to do it."

"Do what?" Jon looked amused at her ramblings.

"You mean you weren't the one who paid off my bracelet?" Christy said slowly. "Then how did you know?"

Jon shook his head and smiled. "I saw the jewelry box sticking out of your purse when you walked by. I knew you'd been making payments on a bracelet at the jewelry store. I figured that must be the one."

"Oh," was all Christy could manage to say.

"Have a good time at Katie's tonight." Jon went back to his stack of bills.

"I will. Thanks." Christy reached for her keys in her purse and headed for her car.

Wait a minute! How did Jon know I was going to Katie's?

Deciding that her boss worked as an undercover

detective in his spare time, Christy unlocked the door
to the small blue car she shared with her mom and slid
onto the seat.

Inside the warm car, she held the bracelet box
solemnly in her hand before opening it. At this
moment it didn't matter who had paid off the balance.
The gold ID bracelet was hers once more.

"Father," she whispered, "thank You. Thank You for
letting me get my bracelet back, and thank You for Todd.
Please keep him safe in Hawaii. And please fix our relationship so I can feel like we're close friends again.
Thank You that You always listen to me, and You care
about every little thing in my life. I love You, Lord."

Opening her eyes, Christy raised the lid on the jewelry box. The instant she saw the bracelet—perfect,
shining, with its engraved "Forever"—she felt jubilant.

Katie could hardly believe Christy's story a short
time later when Christy proudly held out her right arm
for Katie to inspect.

"Do you think Rick paid for it?" Katie asked.

"No, not really. I kind of think it might be my boss,
Jon. He seems like the sort of person who would do
something nice in secret."

"Well, whoever paid for it, I think it's a total God-
thing. I hope you never, ever take it off again."

"I don't plan to," Christy said with a confident
smile. "So, where's Teri? Is she coming?"

"No, she called about an hour ago. I guess her mom
is sick so she thinks she had better stay home and help

out. Looks like it's just you and me."

Katie pointed toward the kitchen table covered with snack food and said, "Do you think we'll have enough to eat?"

"That's not all for us, is it?"

"My mom said my brothers could eat whatever we left, but they're both out with my dad, and they probably won't be back till late. Go ahead and grab some pizza and something to drink. We can eat in the living room. I rented a couple of movies."

Katie sounded as though she was looking forward to their evening together, but Christy could tell Katie was disappointed it was just the two of them.

For the first two hours, they kicked back on the couch, eating and watching an old Disney movie about a VW bug that had a mind of its own. It was kind of funny, but not really.

As soon as the film ended, Christy felt the sadness in Katie's voice again as she said, "Do you want to watch another video or play a game or what?"

"Doesn't matter to me. What do you want to do?

"Are you hungry?" Katie asked. "There's lots more food."

Christy puffed out her cheeks and patted her stomach. "I'm so full I couldn't eat another chip if you forced me."

"We could try new hairstyles," Katie suggested.

"Oh, please! Don't even look at my hair. Ever since the perm went out of mine, and I let my bangs grow, I feel like a ragamuffin. I've given up on my hair. I don't know what to do with it anymore."

"I like it the way it is right now. It looks more like the real you. More natural. No offense, but when you had it short with those poofy bangs, it didn't really fit you, if you know what I mean."

"I used to have really long hair, almost down to my waist," Christy said.

"Why did you cut it?"

"My Aunt Marti talked me into it two summers ago when I first came out from Wisconsin. She told me I needed a California look."

Katie tilted her head, examining Christy's hair. "Yes, I definitely like you better with long hair and without bangs. Didn't you tell me once that Todd said he liked your hair long?"

Christy nodded, smiling at the memory of Todd's comment.

"Speaking of Todd, did you send his card yet?" Katie asked.

"I sent it this morning from work."

"What did you write in it?" Katie asked. "I mean, only if you want to tell me. If it's too personal, that's okay. I understand."

"Don't worry. It was definitely not too personal," Christy said. "I didn't write much. I told him I was praying for him and thinking about him. I told him about my job at the pet store. Stuff like that. I said I hoped he did well in the surfing competitions.

"He's always quoting verses, so I thought I'd send him a verse I liked. Only I just wrote the reference so he'll have to look it up himself."

"That's so cool," Katie said. "It's like sending a message in secret code. What verse was it? Or is that too personal to ask? You don't have to tell me if you don't want to."

"No, it's not too personal. I found it in Philippians, because that's one of my favorite books in the Bible. I don't remember the exact verse. Is your Bible around? I could show you."

Katie uncoiled herself from the couch and returned from her bedroom a moment later with her Bible.

"Here it is," Christy said when she found Philippians. She pointed to chapter 1, verse 3. "Beginning here to the first part of verse 7."

Katie read aloud, "I thank my God in all my remembrance of you, always in every prayer of mine for you all making my prayer with joy, thankful for your partnership in the gospel from the first day until now. And I am sure that he who began a good work in you will bring it to completion at the day of Jesus Christ. It is right for me to feel thus about you all, because I hold you in my heart . . . ."

"Oh, Christy," Katie exclaimed, "that is so romantic!"

"Romantic?" Christy said with a laugh. "It's a Bible verse!"

"I know, but that last part, 'I hold you in my heart,' is so tender. When Todd reads that, he's going to drop his surfboard, hop the next plane, and come running to your doorstep."

Christy laughed. "I doubt it. Hopefully, when Todd reads it, he will feel encouraged and know that I really care about him."

"And that you hold him in your heart," Katie added.

"Oh, stop it, Katie! It's not just about Todd. It says 'you all' a bunch of times. Those verses apply to you too. You're my friend, and I thank God for you all the time."

"I thank God for you too, Christy. It seems that good friends are harder and harder to find." Katie closed her Bible and set it on the coffee table.

"I know what you mean," Christy agreed. "I guess the more things change, the more we have to hold on to true friends."

Katie nodded.

"You know," Christy said, "I'm sorry this didn't turn out to be much of a slumber party, like the ones you used to have. Let's think of something else you and I can do together. What's something you'd really like to do, or somewhere you'd really like to go?"

Katie thought for a moment and said, "Well, there is one thing I've always wanted to do, but I didn't want to do it by myself. I wanted somebody to go with me," Katie said.

"I'll do it with you," Christy said, then quickly added, "as long as it isn't bungee jumping or skydiving."

"No, nothing that wild. It's skiing. I've always

wanted to go skiing."

Christy swallowed hard. To her, skiing was right up there with bungee jumping and all those other sports where you travel at a high speed with no control over your body.

Katie looked at Christy, her freckled nose all scrunched up in anticipation. "So, what do you think? We could join the ski club at school and go on the trip with them to Lake Tahoe at Thanksgiving. Wouldn't that be great? You asked what I really wanted to do, and that's what I've always wanted to do."

Christy knew the believability of her offer to strengthen her friendship with Katie now rested on her answer. Christy knew it was within her power to bless her friend or pull the dream right out from underneath her.

"Is there still time to join the ski club? Haven't they met already?" Christy said, stalling her answer.

"This Monday is the last day to join. They meet after school in Mr. Riley's class. I went last week because I wanted to join, but I didn't particularly want to spend a ski weekend with any of the kids who are in the club."

"You didn't tell me you went," Christy said.

"I didn't think you'd be interested. I guess it was just a wild thought."

"No, it's a great thought. We could do that. We could join the ski club together. I've never been skiing before, though. Do they let people like me join?"

"I've never skied before, either," Katie said. "So I asked last week. They said at Squaw Valley, where they're going for the club trip, they offer ski lessons to beginners like us. We could take ski lessons together."

Katie looked so excited that Christy reluctantly said, "Well, okay. Let's go Monday and sign up."

"This is great!" Katie said, plopping the bowl of M&M's in her lap and tossing a handful into her mouth. "You wait and see. We're going to have the absolute best time! Finally we get to go on a trip together."

Christy tried to ignore all her uncertain, nervous feelings about this. She was doing it for Katie, so it was the right thing to do. She shouldn't be such a chicken when it came to adventure. Hadn't she survived driving the Hana Road this summer in Maui? Certainly she could survive ski lessons.

"What do you want to do now?" Katie asked. "It's only nine-thirty. Do you want to go toilet paper somebody's house? We could give each other egg-white-and-oatmeal facials, maybe. Or we could watch *Gone With the Wind*."

"That's the other movie you rented? You didn't tell me that! I thought it was another 'Love Bug' movie. I'd love to watch *Gone With the Wind*!" Christy exclaimed. "I've only seen it once, and I missed the end because I fell asleep. Let's watch it, okay? I'm not up for going TPing, and what's the point of doing facials when we're stuffing ourselves with junk food?"

Katie jumped up to pop the videocassette into the machine. "So your choice for the evening is a marathon movie and more junk food. I knew there was a reason we got along so well! We have the same taste in slumber parties."

Returning to her nest on the couch, Katie threw her sleeping bag over her legs. She turned to Christy, who now held the candy bowl in her lap, and said, "Come on, future ski bunny. Pass the M&M's."

With a laugh, Christy thought, *Ski chicken is more like it.*

Chapter 4

Friendship? Yes, Please!

How much is this trip going to cost?" Christy's dad asked on Monday evening.

"It's around a hundred dollars, but we're having a fund-raiser so it won't cost that much, really." Christy tried to sound confident. She felt a little more positive about the trip after the meeting that afternoon. It sounded like a lot of fun, and Katie was excited about it.

Christy's dad was on his knees with a screwdriver in his hand, trying to repair the upside-down, disassembled recliner. He scratched his reddish-brown hair with the end of the screwdriver. "That's a lot of money, Christy. How much do you expect to raise, and how are you going to do it?"

"We're selling candy bars for two dollars apiece. A dollar goes toward the cost of the candy, and a dollar toward the trip. Would you like to buy one?" she asked with a childish grin. She knew that her dad could pull the plug on the trip if he didn't think she should go.

"I want a candy bar." David spoke up from his corner of the couch, where he was attempting to do his math homework. "Can I have one?"

"You'll have to ask your mother when she gets back from the grocery store," Dad answered. "She's the one with the secret cash around here. I don't know where she hides it."

"It's in the freezer. I'll show you," David said, scooting off the couch. "She keeps it in that old tin that says 'grease.'"

"Stay where you are, son. Get that homework done."

Dad went back to work on the chair, muttering to himself, "Imagine that, all these years, and I never knew where she kept it. Even my ten-year-old knows that what I thought was frozen bacon grease was really her stash."

Just then the phone rang and David jumped up. "I'll get it!"

"Don't bother, David, I've already got it," Christy said, reaching for the wall phone in the kitchen.

"Christina, dear," came the voice on the other end. "How are you? Bob and I were just saying we hadn't heard from you for a while and wondered how everything was going there."

"We're all fine, Aunt Marti. How are you guys?"

"We're both fine. How's school going for you? Are you finding new groups to get involved with since you dropped out of cheerleading?"

Christy cringed at the jab about cheerleading, but

she was glad to report to her aunt that she had joined the ski club. She knew that was the kind of club Aunt Marti would approve of.

That news was all Aunt Marti needed to set into motion a string of plans. First she told Christy she would take three boxes of the fund-raiser candy bars and sell them at her next women's meeting. Whatever portion of the necessary one hundred dollars Christy couldn't raise, Aunt Marti would gladly supply.

Of course, Christy couldn't go skiing without the right attire. Aunt Marti said she would go shopping tomorrow for ski clothes and have the outfits sent directly to Christy's house.

"The clothes should arrive this weekend at the latest," Aunt Marti stated. "That should give you plenty of time to try them on and decide if you need any more."

"Aunt Marti, you really don't have to do all this for me, you know."

"Why are you always trying to spoil my fun, Christina? You know I love helping you out like this. Goodness knows, your mother would love to provide these things for you, if she could. But we all know that's just not possible on your father's salary. Let me do this for you and please, stop acting as if it's such a huge favor. It's nothing, really."

Christy sighed. She learned long ago not to cross her aunt. "Thanks, Aunt Marti. Do you want me to mail the boxes of candy to you or what?"

"Actually, Bob is playing golf in Rancho Santa Fe

this Wednesday. I'll have him stop by and pick up the candy. I might even be able to send some of the ski clothes with him. That is, if I can find everything we need by tomorrow. Say, is your mother home? I need to talk to her."

"She just walked in the door," Christy said, lifting the phone cord so her mom could walk under it.

Mom's round face looked flushed as she placed two big bags of groceries on the counter and brushed back her short, graying hair.

"It's your sister," Christy said, handing Mom the phone.

Mom smiled, took the phone, and answered brightly, "Hello, Martha. How are you?"

With her free hand, Mom motioned for Christy to unload the rest of the groceries.

"Come on, David," Christy called as she marched through the living room. "Help me carry in the groceries."

"I can't," David said, pushing up his glasses. "I have to finish my homework."

Oh, brother, Christy thought, *you'll jump up to answer the phone and to reveal Mom's freezer secrets, but when I ask you to help, you suddenly have to do your homework.*

"Go on, David," Dad said. "You can take a quick break and help your sister. I think I'll take a break too." He laid down the screwdriver and joined Christy and David in unloading the car.

A few minutes later the kitchen counters were covered with six bags of groceries. Mom had hung up the phone and begun the challenge of putting everything away.

"How come you never buy any good stuff?" David asked. "All my friends at school get cupcakes and candy bars in their lunches. All I ever get is an oatmeal cookie."

"I'm trying to keep our family healthy," Mom said. "We all eat too much junk food as it is. I'm not going to pay good money for that stuff when a homemade oatmeal cookie is much better for you."

Dad turned to Christy and said under his breath, "Sounds like your mother read another one of those health-food articles. Just watch. Bet you anything we're having tofu and bean sprouts for dinner."

"I heard that," Mom said. "And no, we're not having tofu. We're having stir-fry."

"With beef?" Dad asked, looking hopeful.

"No."

"Chicken?"

"No, just vegetables. Lots and lots of vegetables."

Dad looked disappointed.

Mom tried to convince him. "We don't need to eat meat at every meal. Besides, it saves money on our food bill, and it's good for us to pork out on vegetables every once in a while."

"Pork," Dad repeated. "Now that's a good idea. You could throw some pork chops in with those vegetables, and we'd have a real meal."

Mom gave Dad a look Christy knew well. It was a mock-stern look in which she stuck out her chin and lowered her eyebrows. But all it did was make Dad laugh.

"Okay, okay," Dad said. In two steps he was across the kitchen floor and scooping up Mom in a bear hug.

"We'll be your vegetarian guinea pigs tonight. And tomorrow night, if you want to test out a huge slab of prime rib on us, hey, we won't complain a bit, will we kids?"

"Yeesh," David said. "They look like they're going to start kissing. I'm going to do my homework."

Christy kept putting away the groceries. Out of the corner of her eye she watched her parents snuggling. She thought it was kind of cute the way they still teased each other and acted a little goofy, especially after being married for so many years.

"Oh, leave those out," Mom said when she saw Christy loading the celery and carrots into the refrigerator. "That's part of our stir-fry for tonight."

"I'll leave you two to your chop-sueying," Dad said, heading back to his project in the living room. He still had a grin on his face.

Christy thought of how her dad came across so gruff and stern most of the time. Then, at moments like this, she wondered what he was like as a teenager and what her mom was like when the two of them first met.

While they spent the next twenty minutes chopping

up vegetables, Christy asked her mom questions about how she met Dad and what things were like for them. Most of Mom's answers Christy had already heard. She knew the stories of their engagement and wedding by heart.

"What about when you were dating?" Christy asked. "What made you so sure you liked Dad more than that other guy you were dating? What was his name? Chuck?"

"Well, you know, in a small town everyone knows everyone else," Mom explained. "I had known your father since we were in grade school. The other kids said he was a bully because he was kind of big for his age. I thought he was shy, though. And I liked him as a good friend for many years."

Mom opened a new bottle of canola oil and poured some into the hot electric skillet. "So, when he finally asked me out, it just seemed right because we'd been friends—good friends—for so many years."

"How did you know he was the one you wanted to marry?" Christy asked, scraping the carrots off the cutting board and watching them dance into the hot skillet.

Mom's worry lines disappeared, and she said, "Because I couldn't picture myself spending the rest of my life with anyone else."

Christy thought about her mom's statement for the rest of the evening. After dinner she attacked her homework. The first paper she pulled out was her

English essay on true friends. The class had slid by without them having to turn in their essays that morning because they had had a substitute who didn't know anything about the assignment.

The night before, Christy had thrown away her first draft and put together a couple of paragraphs on how a true friend was someone you can trust. Reading her essay now, it sounded flat.

"A true friend is . . . ," she repeated, lifting her stuffed Pooh Bear and balancing him on her knees. "What is a true friend, Pooh?"

Deciding to work from what she already had written rather than start over, Christy continued to write about how you can always trust a true friend. She thought it would be nice to include Katie in her essay since Katie seemed to be writing about her.

"A true friend will tell you what you need to hear," Christy wrote, "even when what she or he has to say may not be what you want to hear."

After several minutes of work, Christy reread her essay and started to critique her grammar. She wondered if it was okay to end one of her sentences with *is*. She knew the teacher would squawk because she had used the word *totally*, so she changed it to *sincerely*.

Then she noticed she had used *sincerely* a few words later. Using the same word twice, so close together, was another no-no with her English teacher.

This is a lot harder than I thought it would be. But I sure could use a good grade in this class.

It took her at least fifteen minutes to rewrite her sentences. By the time she had finished, she had lost any previous creativity.

I don't think it's possible for my right brain and left brain to work together. How can I be creative and critical at the same time? This writing business is hard!

Forcing herself to go on, Christy tried extra hard to capture a good description of a friend. It seemed to take forever. She decided that writing three full pages was entirely too long an assignment for such a simple topic.

At least Christy had nice handwriting in her favor. When she finally finished, she recopied the paper so it would look neat. She liked the final line of her essay, "I would have to agree with Constantine, who said, 'My treasures are my friends.' " It was her favorite quote from the list her English teacher had passed out.

"What do you think, Pooh Bear?" Christy asked, holding up her finished paper for him to see. "Think I'll get an A?"

Christy tucked her paper into her notebook and got ready for bed. Before turning out the light, she reached under her bed and pulled out a shoe box covered in green and mauve floral paper. She opened it and peered at the three letters inside.

This was her secret box, containing letters written to her future husband. She wrote the first letter on her sixteenth birthday. The other two she wrote during the past few months when she had something on her heart she wanted to write down for the guy she would some-day marry.

Every time she wrote to him, she prayed for him. Her goal was to present this box to her husband on their wedding day. He would see that for years she had been praying for him and thinking about how she could be the best partner in the world for him.

Christy lifted the pad of plain, white writing paper and in her best handwriting wrote,

Dear future husband,

I was thinking today about friends and about how I want us to always be good friends—before and after we're married. I think I still have a lot to learn about how to be a good friend, but I'm trying to be more encouraging and supportive of my friend Katie. I actually let her talk me into going skiing! Do you like to ski?

I just wanted you to know I'm praying for you and thinking about you.

Your friend,

Christy

She carefully folded the letter and added it to the collection in the box. Then, slipping the box back under her bed, she held Pooh Bear tight and prayed for her future husband—whomever and wherever he might be.

Chapter 5

Way to Go, Katie!

On Wednesday, Christy hurried home from school and finished her homework before dinner. Her youth group met on Wednesday nights for Bible study, and the agreement with her parents was that she had to have her homework done before she could go. She had only been to the Bible study once before, because she had never managed to complete her homework in time. Tonight she had a good reason for going—Katie.

Christy grabbed her Bible and car keys, eager to rush out the door at ten minutes before seven. Her mom called after her, "Be sure you're home by nine. Don't give anyone a ride. Lock the doors, and call us if you have any problems."

"Okay, Mom," Christy answered. "I'll be fine. See you at nine."

Smiling to herself she thought, *I'm only going a few miles to church. My parents make it sound as though I'm going on a safari!*

She made it just in time and found Katie in the back row, saving a seat for her.

"Did you see that new guy over there?" Katie whis-

44

pered, pointing toward the front of the room. "He just moved here from Ecuador. I heard his parents are missionaries."

Christy saw the guy Katie was pointing to. He was nice-looking with light brown hair, broad shoulders, and fair-colored skin with a sprinkling of freckles.

"He sure doesn't look like a missionary kid," Christy whispered back.

"Why? Because he looks normal?" Katie asked.

"I guess. You know what I mean. He looks like any other guy here."

"Let's talk to him afterward, okay? I bet it's not easy to make friends and fit into a new culture and everything after living in the jungle."

"Did he really live in the jungle?" Christy asked.

"Sure! Where else would a missionary live in Ecuador?"

The Bible study leader, Luke, asked everyone to find a seat so they could get started.

Christy watched the new guy sit down in the front row and thought, *That missionary kid doesn't look like the Tarzan-type. I wonder if he really lived in a rain forest?*

After opening in prayer, Luke introduced Glen to the rest of the group and had him stand and say a few words.

Glen looked nervous as he quickly explained that he and his family were missionaries in the city of Quito and that his dad worked at a Christian radio station there.

Christy and Katie exchanged glances and Katie

whispered, "And I thought he lived in a hut and ate tree bark!"

The study that night centered on what it meant to be a missionary. At least four times Luke said, "Each of us is a missionary right where we are. We don't have to go to a foreign country to tell others about the Lord. Start seeing your high school as your mission field." Toward the end he asked if anyone had any comments to add.

To Christy's surprise, Katie's hand shot up.

"I want to ask you guys to pray for us—for Christy and me—because we're sort of going on a missions trip."

Christy gave Katie a puzzled look, feeling a little embarrassed that Katie had included her name in this announcement, especially since she wasn't sure what Katie was getting at.

With a grin Katie explained to the group, "We've joined the ski club at Kelley High, and we're going on a trip with them over Thanksgiving weekend. I think it's going to be a real opportunity to witness to a lot of the people, because they're not really the type who would go to church."

"That's great!" Luke said. "It's a chance for you both to see what it's like to be in the world but not of it. We'll be praying for you both."

He turned around and wrote on the board, "Katie Weldon and Christy Miller—school ski trip."

"Does anyone else have something they'd like to add?"

I wonder what he meant by "in the world but not of it"? This ski trip is such a big deal for Katie! Now she's turned it into a missions trip. I hope she doesn't get too disappointed if it ends up we can't go.

"I have something," said a girl in the middle of the room.

Christy had seen her before, but she went to a different school, and Christy didn't know her name. She seemed really nice. Christy had thought once before when she saw her in Sunday school that she was the kind of girl Christy would like to get to know.

"Sure, Lisa, go ahead," Luke said.

"I have a list I started a couple of weeks ago, and I've been carrying it around in the back of my Bible. I guess you could call it a hit list."

Some people sitting near Lisa laughed. She didn't look like the kind of person who would have a hit list. Tall and gentle-looking, Lisa had long, brown hair that hung in soft curls. She appeared to be the sort of person who had a kind word for everyone.

Lisa's cheeks began to turn pink as she explained, "It's not a list of people I'm trying to get . . ." She paused and said, "Well, I guess maybe it is."

Lisa looked flustered. Luke jumped in and encouraged her to keep going. "That's okay," he said. "I think I know what you're getting at. A hit list is probably the best way of describing it too. Go ahead and explain what the list is for."

Looking a little more courageous, Lisa went on.

"See, what I did was ask God to show me who He wanted me to witness to this year at school. Then, when certain friends came to mind, I wrote down their names. I have six names on my list, and every night when I have my quiet time I pray for them."

"Is your plan to simply pray for these six friends?" Luke asked.

"Well, I really wanted to start witnessing to my friends, but I wasn't sure exactly how to do it. A couple of weeks ago you taught about how prayer is the key that unlocks any door. So I'm starting by praying for them. Then, when opportunities come up, I want to tell them about the Lord."

"That's a great idea, Lisa," Luke said. "Let me ask you something. Do you feel it's your personal responsibility to make sure each one of those six friends gives his or her heart to the Lord?"

Christy thought of how she might answer if Luke had directed the question toward her. She probably would have said "yes." It seemed to her that if she were willing to make that kind of commitment to pray for six friends, then she should be willing to keep at it until they all became Christians.

"No," Lisa answered.

You're a lot braver than I am, Lisa, to admit that in front of everybody!

"I mean, I feel it's my personal responsibility to pray for them every day and to tell them about the Lord. But I know the way they respond to it all is their own responsibility."

"Good," Luke said. "I'm glad you see the difference. That's what witnessing is all about. We need to be faithful to pray and faithful to share, but we must leave all the results up to God. If we've done all that, and they're still not interested, we have to try not to take it personally. If they reject the message, remember, it's our heavenly Father they're rejecting."

Luke turned and added Lisa Huisman's name to the list on the board.

"We'll be praying for you, too, on your missionary journey. I'd encourage all of you to start your own hit list. Remember, the foundation has to be prayer." Luke took a deep breath and crossed his arms across his broad chest.

Then he looked at his watch and said, "We need to wrap it up. Let's pray for Katie, Christy, and Lisa."

Luke prayed for them and then closed the Bible study by saying, "Everyone, be sure to introduce yourself to Glen. One more thing. There's a sign-up sheet at the back door for the Pizza Feed, Friday night after the football game. It's three dollars for church kids and free for any friends you bring."

Everyone started to talk. Luke spoke over the rumblings. "This is exactly what we've been talking about, you guys. A chance to bring your friends to a place where they'll hear about the Lord and have fun at the same time. Don't just come by yourself or with your church friends. Consider this your missionary opportunity of the week."

Then, sounding like a football coach, Luke shouted, "Now everybody go out there and give 'em heaven this week!"

Christy felt bad because she had to work Friday night and couldn't come to the Pizza Feed. The whole lesson that night had made her think, though, about how few nonChristian friends she had. If she were going to the Pizza Feed, who would she invite? Maybe this ski club was a good idea because she could meet some people who weren't Christians and invite them to church with her.

"Come on," Katie urged, standing up and tugging on Christy's arm. "Let's meet Glen."

"Do I detect a girl with a crush on a guy here?" Christy teased.

"I'm only trying to be friendly," Katie said with a gleam in her eye. "Luke told us to make Glen feel welcome, didn't he?"

Just then Luke came up and said, "I'm glad you told us about the ski club, Katie. It's a great opportunity for both of you."

His warm smile made Christy feel welcomed into the group as he turned to her and said, "I'm glad to see you here, Christy. I hope it works out for you to come all the time."

"Yeah, it should," Christy said, feeling a little guilty for not becoming involved earlier. "I wanted to come to the Pizza Feed on Friday, but I have to work."

"Maybe you can stop by after work," Luke suggested. "We'll be cranked up here until around midnight."

Christy felt silly explaining to Luke that her parents had a strict curfew of ten o'clock. She smiled and said, "Maybe."

Katie looked over Christy's shoulder, obviously trying to track Glen. "We probably should get going, Christy," Katie said.

"Can I ask you both a question first?" Luke asked.

Katie glanced over at Glen and then back at Luke. "Yeah?"

"Do either of you see Rick Doyle anymore? I thought someone said he was dating one of you."

"Not me!" Katie said in quick defense.

Christy shyly admitted, "I was. I went out with him last month. He isn't around anymore, though, because he's going to San Diego State."

"I knew that," Luke said, "but I was trying to see if he was spending time with any Christians. He sort of dropped out of everything toward the end of last year, and I haven't seen him around. I thought I'd see who keeps in contact with him and find out how he's doing."

"I don't really know much about how he's doing," Christy said. "But he moved into an apartment with some Christian guys, and one of them, Doug, is a friend of mine. Doug's a real strong Christian."

"Well, good. That's encouraging," Luke said. "If you see Rick, tell him I asked about him and that I'm praying for him."

"She probably won't see him," Katie blurted out, giving Christy a "let's-get-going" look. Then quickly she added, "I need to sign up for the Pizza Feed. Excuse me." With a swish of her copper hair, she turned and made a beeline for the clipboard by the back door.

Christy noticed Glen by the door with pen in hand, ready to sign up, when Katie practically pounced on him. She must have said something funny to him, because he smiled at her, and they began a conversation.

Way to go, Katie!

Christy glanced at the clock on the wall and realized she only had ten minutes to make it home by nine. She caught Katie's eye, waved good-bye, and headed for the less-crowded front door.

All the way home she thought how cute it was seeing Katie with a crush on Glen. She hoped he was a nice guy and wouldn't break her heart. She couldn't wait till the next day at school so she could ask Katie how everything went with him.

"Okay, so tell me your opening line," Christy said the next morning when she entered her English class and found Katie already at her desk.

"What opening line?"

"With Glen! You had him laughing in ten seconds. How did you do it?"

"Oh, that," Katie said with a laugh. "You noticed, huh?"

"Yes, of course I noticed. Tell me what happened."

"I just asked him if he ever ate bug larvae in Ecuador."

"Katie, how gross!" But Christy had to giggle. "Why did you ask him that?"

"I wanted to be original," Katie said with a smile. "It worked! He said he'd look for me tomorrow night at the Pizza Feed."

The teacher interrupted their conversation by saying, "This is not a social club. Will you please find your seat, Miss Miller, so we can begin our class?"

Why do I get the feeling this teacher isn't exactly crazy about me?

Christy hurried to her seat and made a special effort to perform as a model student for the remainder of the class.

At lunch Christy caught up on the rest of Katie's story. It sounded as though she and Glen really hit it off, and Katie was excited about seeing him Friday night. Christy felt a little left out since she had to work. She determined to be enthusiastic and supportive of Katie, the same way Katie had always been supportive of her.

"What do you think I should wear?" Katie asked. "Jeans would probably be good, right? And what? A sweatshirt or sweater or T-shirt? I could wear that University of Hawaii one you got me, or is that too cheesy?"

"No, I think that would be great."

"You're just saying that. I can tell. Your words are

saying, 'That's great,' but your face is saying, 'Katie, girl, go buy yourself a new shirt.' And can I just say that I think that's a very good idea and that you have been elected to come shopping with me to help pick it out?"

Katie caught her breath and looked at Christy expectantly. "How about it? Can you go to the mall after school?"

"I don't know. I'll have to ask. If you think about it, you already have some really nice outfits you could wear, if you didn't have the money to buy something new." Christy chose her words carefully, since a few weeks ago Katie had said that all she had to spend on back-to-school clothes was fifty dollars her grandmother had sent her and that had barely paid for her tennis shoes.

"I've got twenty dollars from baby-sitting that I was going to use for the ski trip. This seems much more important, though."

"How are you doing on selling your candy bars?" Christy asked. "Do you think you'll sell ten boxes in the next three weeks?"

Katie quickly turned the question back on Christy. "How about you? How many have you sold so far?"

"Well, my uncle came by last night while we were at youth group. He was going to take three of the boxes for my aunt to sell at her women's group."

"So, you made thirty dollars without doing a thing? Without even being home?"

"Actually, he ended up taking all ten boxes. He said

he'd pass them out to all the trick-or-treaters on Halloween."

"Let me get this straight," Katie said. "Your uncle bought all ten of your boxes last night, and now you have your total amount for the ski trip raised?"

"Well . . . yeah, I guess I do." It hadn't hit Christy that way until this minute. She now had even fewer reasons to back out of the trip.

"All you need is for your aunt to buy you a couple of new ski outfits, and you're all set."

"I told you she was doing that, right?"

Katie threw her hands up in the air. "Don't tell me. She already bought you a new outfit."

"Come on. I told you she was going to buy some ski stuff, at least I thought I told you."

Christy couldn't believe how upset Katie was acting over Uncle Bob and Aunt Marti's generous involvement. "My uncle left the outfits last night, but I haven't tried them on yet."

"Christy, I was being sarcastic about the outfits! You mean your aunt actually bought you some?"

"You have to understand what my aunt is like. This is nothing to her. It's her way of being a part of my life, or something. It's not like I go around asking her to buy me things."

Katie shook her head. "You are spoiled rotten by your rich relatives, Christy Miller, and you don't even know it."

Now it was Christy's turn to get huffy. "I am not! I

have to work just so I can have money to put gas in the car. Did you forget that? And you've seen where I live. My family can't even afford to buy a house; we're renting that little house. Your house is three times as big as ours, you have your own car, and your dad pays for your insurance and your gas."

"Okay, okay." Katie bowed her head in surrender. "You're right. This is ridiculous for us to get all hyper over nothing. I guess I didn't expect you to have your money this soon, especially when I'm dealing with negative funds . . ." Her voice trailed off.

"What do you mean?" Christy asked.

"I kind of, well, I sort of haven't sold any, really."

"Wait a minute," Christy said, reaching for Katie's fund-raiser candy box next to her and opening the cardboard handle. "There are only two left in here. That means you sold eight. That's eight dollars toward the trip. What's wrong with that?"

Katie's voice became softer as she looked down and said, "I didn't exactly sell eight candy bars."

Christy counted again. "There are only two left in here. With ten in a box, that means you sold eight, right? You've earned eight dollars."

Looking up and biting her lower lip, Katie confessed, "Actually, I owe sixteen dollars."

Christy's blue-green eyes widened, and she said, "Katie Weldon, you didn't!"

"Well, see, I have this thing about chocolate. I can't be in the same room with it. It starts calling my name, and it says, 'Eat me! Eat me!' In the middle of the night, it wakes me up. When I'm trying to do my homework, it keeps bothering me. Really, Christy, I've tried ignoring it. I've tried telling myself that it's calling to some other Katie, not me. I've tried everything! The only way to shut it up is to eat it."

By this time Christy was giggling at Katie's confession. "Eight jumbo chocolate bars in two days?"

"Three days," Katie corrected. "We got them on Monday, remember?"

"Aren't you sick?"

"Actually, I feel pretty good," Katie said, her mischievous smile returning. "I kind of feel like I'm in love. Isn't that what they said in science last year? Chocolate releases some chemical in your brain and makes you think you're in love?"

"I don't know about that, but you'd better lay off the candy bars tonight and tomorrow. Otherwise, when you see Glen tomorrow night you won't know if it's true love or the chocolate double-crossing you!"

"I think you're right," Katie said somberly. "What should I do about the fund-raiser, though? I mean, this is like the worst-case scenario possible. We're supposed to go on this trip together, and so far, you have all your money, as well as new outfits, and I owe the ski club sixteen bucks. You wouldn't go skiing without me, would you?"

Christy laughed some more before offering her solution. "How about if you give me all your chocolate bars, and I'll see if we can sell them at the pet shop? Jon is cool about stuff like this. Then, instead of buying a new shirt for tomorrow night, why don't you borrow one of mine so you'll feel like you're wearing something new? Then give me sixteen of your twenty dollars so your fund-raiser account will be brought back up to zero."

"I suppose you're right. That only leaves me with four dollars, though."

"So? That will get you through the weekend. The Pizza Feed costs three dollars, and you have a dollar left over for . . . for offering on Sunday!"

"Good idea," Katie said. "I was thinking of giving to a special church fund, anyway."

"Let me guess," Christy said. "Could it be the missionary fund?"

Both girls started to laugh.

"You know, those missionaries need all the support they can get," Katie said.

"And I'm sure you'll see to that by socially supporting your very own favorite missionary tomorrow night!" Christy teased.

"We all must try to do whatever we can," Katie said with a mock straight face. "And this is my little way of helping out."

Chapter 6

Peculiar Treasures

That afternoon Katie and Christy set out to find a shirt of Christy's for Katie to borrow. Forty-five minutes into the project, Christy's bed was covered with clothes, and Katie still hadn't decided on one. She had tried on nearly everything Christy owned, but nothing seemed to suit her.

"I still like the green one on you," Christy commented, lowering herself to the floor and resting her back against her bed.

Katie held it up and gave her honest opinion. "It looks like old-fashioned long underwear."

"I know. It's supposed to. It looks good on you."

Katie slipped it back on and studied herself in the mirror. "But it's long-sleeved. What if it's really hot inside?"

"Push up the sleeves. Yeah, like that. It looks sporty on you."

"I always look sporty. I don't want to look sporty; I want to look cute. No, take that back. I want to look attractive. No, change that to stunning. No, actually. . ."

Katie spun around and spurted out, "I don't want to

59

look like me; I want to look like you!"

"Like me?" Christy stammered. "Why? You're adorable, Katie. Look at you. You've got the total aerobic body; unique, red, swishy hair; and wildly green eyes. I mean it, Katie; you're adorable."

"I don't want green eyes. I want guys to call them 'killer eyes,' like they do yours. And unique red hair is great only when you're a groupie at a rock concert. I'd rather have shiny brown hair like yours."

Christy was silent. She had never compared herself to Katie before, and she didn't know how to deny the things Katie was saying about her.

"Face it," Katie said, letting her true feelings out. "With your looks and your personality, you have guys like Rick and Todd clamoring for your attention. Not me. I've never had a guy be even slightly interested in me. Remember the disaster last year when I asked a guy to the prom?"

Christy nodded in sympathy, remembering Katie's green carnation corsage and the way Lance had ignored her all night and then sent her home alone in his rented limo.

"Who am I kidding?" Katie asked, slumping onto the floor next to Christy. "Why do I think Glen would be interested in me?"

"Because you're you," Christy said. "You're wonderful, and God made you a peculiar treasure."

"A what?"

"My grandma used to say that. She showed it to me

in her Bible once. It's in the Old Testament somewhere. Exodus, I think. God called His people His
'peculiar treasure.' That's what you are, Katie. That's
what we both are—God's peculiar treasures. So what if
there isn't a guy in your life yet who appreciates you
for who you are? Just keep being yourself and hold out
for a hero, okay?"

Tears brimmed in Katie's eyes as she leaned over and
gave Christy a hug. "If I didn't have you as my closest
friend, Christy, I would be totally miserable!"

"No, no, no," Christy said. "It's the other way
around. If *I* didn't have *you* as my closest friend, I'd be
totally miserable."

"I guess we're just a pair of unmiserable peculiar
treasures," Katie said with a laugh.

"And this unmiserable peculiar treasure," Christy
said, pointing at Katie, "is going to look adorable
tomorrow night in an old-fashioned, long-underwear,
green shirt with the sleeves pushed up. And she is
going to be herself, and she is going to have a wonderful time!"

"If you say so," Katie said, her grin returning.
Glancing at all the clothes on the bed, she teased, "Are
you sure there's nothing else I can try on?"

"Oh, wait here. As a matter of fact, there is! I'll be
right back."

Christy scurried out of the room and returned a
moment later with three big shopping bags. "The ski
outfits from Aunt Marti," she announced.

The two friends laughingly tore into the bags and were soon modeling the bright-colored skiwear.

"Are these pants bright or what?" Katie asked, checking out the hot pink and black swirl-patterned ski pants in the mirror. A black turtleneck with hot pink squiggles on the neck and cuffs completed the outfit. "I don't know if I could actually wear this in public."

"Here," Christy said, lifting a pair of black snow pants from the last bag. "These are pretty basic. Why don't you try these instead of those swirl-woman pants?"

"Good idea. I'm sure these would look much better on you. I'm not exactly the hot-pink-super-heroine-type," Katie said, handing over the wild swirl pants and matching turtleneck.

Christy tried them on. She felt flashy and daring. She decided that looking the part of an experienced skier might be half the battle in persuading herself to actually hit the slopes. Yes, she would definitely keep the hot pink outfit.

"That looks much better on you," Katie said, pulling on the black ski pants. "These fit me pretty well. What do you think? Could I borrow them for the trip?"

"Of course. Here, try on this sweater." Christy tossed Katie a white sweater with black triangles woven across the yoke and shoulders. "That looks great together, and the colors are good with your hair."

"Look at us," Katie said, examining their reflections in the full-length mirror. "We look like we know how to ski already. Hand me those black gloves."

Christy scooped up the new gloves off the floor and grabbed a pair of ski goggles from the bottom of a bag.

Katie put on the gloves and goggles, and striking a ski pose, she shouted, "Look out, Lake Tahoe! A couple of peculiar treasures are coming your way!"

Aunt Marti called later that night to see if Christy liked any of the new ski clothes.

"They're all great, and they fit. I'm going to let Katie borrow the black pants and matching sweater, if that's okay," Christy said.

"Well then, will you still have enough outfits? You're going to be there an entire weekend," Marti said.

"I'm sure I won't need anything else."

"I'll pick up another pair of the black ski pants and a red sweater to go with them. I almost bought the red sweater the other day, but I remembered how you once told me that Rick liked you in red. I didn't want to make you feel bad, since you broke up with the poor guy. But since you do need another outfit, I'll go ahead and get the red sweater. Just know, Christy dear, that I'm not buying it to remind you of Rick."

Oh, brother; did my aunt totally ditch "tact school" or what?

"I appreciate the outfits, Aunt Marti. You don't have to get me anything else, though. Really."

"Nonsense! I'll send the pants and sweater tomorrow, and I'll send an extra pair of goggles for your friend."

"Thank you, Aunt Marti. And tell Uncle Bob thanks for buying all the candy bars."

"Oh, he's sitting here at the kitchen table right now, sticking orange pumpkin labels on them. You know your uncle. He likes to have a special treat for the kids around here on Halloween. Are you going to dress up this year?"

"I don't think so."

"We really should throw a costume party for you next year. Wouldn't that be fun? When I was your age, your mother and I had a costume party, and I dressed up like a flapper."

"You dressed up like Flipper the dolphin?"

"No, dear, I said a flapper. You know, a dancer from the Roaring Twenties. I probably still have the costume. Well, you think about it and decide when we should have that party for you. It could be a fun welcome-home party for Todd. You don't know when he's coming back yet, do you?"

Christy swallowed hard. "No, I don't know."

"I see. Well, all in good time. I want you to know I'm very proud of you for joining this ski club. It'll give you a chance to meet other young people, and as stylish as you're going to look, who knows what might happen!"

Right! Who knows? I might break every bone in my body. But thanks to you, Aunt Marti, I'll look stylish doing it.

The next day at work, Christy asked Jon about selling the candy bars for Katie.

"Fine with me. Put a sign on the box, and don't

leave them where a kid could walk off with one," Jon suggested. "How much do they cost?"

"Two dollars each. There are ten in each box," Christy explained.

"Really?" Jon's expression brightened. "I'll take a box."

"A whole box? For yourself?"

"No, for my sister. She's a chocaholic. I'll send her a box for her birthday. Saves me having to decide what to get for her. And it's already boxed. This will be easier than trying to mail the vase or the perfume."

Jon lifted one of the boxes of chocolate from Christy's shopping bag and pulled a twenty-dollar bill out of his pocket. "Thanks, Christy. You made my life a little easier today!"

Christy looked at the easy twenty and then back at Jon. "It was nothing, really. Glad to help out." She pulled an envelope from her purse and stuck the twenty-dollar bill in along with the sixteen dollars Katie had given her for the eight bars she ate.

Katie, we just might end up going on this ski trip, after all. Only eighty-two more bars to go!

Finding some felt pens on a shelf in the back, Christy made up a sign for the box of candy bars and took them out front to the register. Beverly was standing there, handing change back to a customer.

"Hi," Christy said. "I'm going to put this up here. Jon said it was okay."

"Smells like chocolate," Beverly said. "A very welcome change of fragrance from the usual pet store smells. They should sell well here. Jon left for a few minutes. He said he was going to mail his sister's birthday present. I forgot to ask if he ended up deciding on the perfume or the vase."

"Neither," Christy said. "He's sending her a box of chocolate bars."

Beverly laughed and shook her head. Her long braid wiggled down her back like a little girl's jump rope. "You never can tell with that guy. What did I tell you? The king of returns. Watch, he'll take back the vase and the perfume, and he'll buy something else. What do you think it'll be?"

"A tie, maybe?" Christy guessed.

"No, I've never seen him wear a tie," said Beverly. "Maybe he'll get a leather belt or something wild, like one of those new Billings Cycle Machines. It's an exercise bike and stair-step machine in one. He's been talking about keeping one in the back so he could exercise in his spare time."

"What spare time?" Christy asked. "The guy never stops!"

"Oh, there's the phone. I'll get it. Are you ready to take over the register?"

"Sure," said Christy. She watched Beverly hotfoot it to the back room and thought of how little she knew about Beverly and Jon. They both seemed like nice, low-stress people.

But where did they stand with the Lord? After

Luke's talk at the Wednesday night Bible study and Lisa's "hit list," Christy felt concerned about finding ways to be a missionary to those around her.

During her break, she made a quick trip to the small Bible bookstore at the other end of the mall. She bought two little booklets that told how to become a Christian and a card for Katie that said, "Our God is an awesome God."

Back at the pet store, she tried to decide the best way to deliver the booklets to Beverly and Jon. She thought about casually leaving them at the back table. That seemed chicken. Maybe she should personally hand the booklets to them and say something like, "This is regarding life and death. Please read it." No, that sounded too dramatic.

By the time she left work that night, she had worked herself into a frazzle, trying to figure out how to deliver her urgent witnessing message. She had thought of at least twenty different ways to give them to Jon and Beverly, but she had said none of them, and the booklets were still in her purse.

I hope Katie had more success on her mission tonight than I did, Christy thought as she fell into bed.

Katie called the next morning at nine-thirty with a mixed report.

"He kind of talked to me. Sort of. It was weird. It was like neither of us knew what to talk about, so we just sat there. It was pretty noisy, so it was hard to have a conversation. But he sat by me for most of the time.

Actually, he sat across from me. He didn't say anything about seeing me on Sunday or next Wednesday. I
guess he was just being polite."

"Or," Christy suggested, "he was nervous and
didn't know what to say. Did you ever think of that?
Guys can get nervous, too, you know."

"I don't know," Katie said. "I saw him talking to a
bunch of guys in the parking lot before we went in, and
he was real yakity-yak with them. Then he came in and
sat across from me and hardly said anything."

"Don't you see? He was talking to *guys* out front.
Guys, Katie. That's different than trying to talk to a
girl. Especially a girl he's interested in. I'm sure Glen
was nervous, and that's why he didn't talk much."

"You think so?"

"Yes. Look at all the positive things that happened.
He left a bunch of guys and came over and sat by you."

"I hadn't thought of that," Katie said.

"Right there is proof, I think, that he's interested in
you. And the second thing is that he stayed for a while.
He could've left at any time. I think he stayed because
he wanted to. He was being shy or nervous or unsure of
himself. I think in another setting, maybe where it's
quieter, Glen will open up more."

"I hope you're right, Christy. He seems like a neat
guy with a real tender heart. I hope we have another
chance to talk sometime."

"You will. I'm sure you will. I think it went well for
your first time together. You'll probably see him on

Sunday. What are you going to wear?"

"Don't make any jokes, but I think I'll wear a dress," Katie said. "I know it'll be the first time most of my friends have ever seen me in anything other than shorts or jeans. It could be a little mind-boggling for some. They'll probably think Katie's long-lost twin is visiting the youth department. But, hey, sometimes you have to step out and be a little brave."

"Speaking of being a little brave," Christy said, "I was planning on witnessing to Jon and Beverly last night at work, only nothing happened. I guess Glen wasn't the only one who was too nervous and shy to speak up."

"Wait until there's a natural opportunity to say something. It'll work out," Katie said.

"And it'll work out for you too. With Glen, I mean. You wait for a natural opportunity to say something to him too."

"There's nothing in the rule book that says I can't wait in a dress, is there?"

Christy laughed. "Nope. I think the dress will be a nice touch."

Later Christy wondered what might add a nice touch to her witnessing attempt. Maybe a card from the Bible bookstore with a verse on it. That way she could slip the booklet inside the card and seal the envelope.

The morning at work went fast, because they were busy doing a lot of restocking in the store. For the first hour, Christy ended up in the back, opening and marking boxes of pet food.

During her lunch break, she made a quick trip to the Bible bookstore. For twenty minutes she scanned every card on the rack. None of them seemed to be just right for Jon and Beverly.

In the end, Christy bought two cards that had garden scenes on the front of them and were blank inside. She thought she would have better success thinking up her own message.

All afternoon she ran ideas through her mind, trying to come up with the right phrase for the witnessing cards. Only snappy lines came to mind. It was as if she was trying to enter some Christian bumper-sticker contest or something.

Have you considered your eternal destiny lately?
Did you know heaven is just a prayer away?
Get right or get left!
Here's a word from our Heavenly Sponsor.
Please don't die without God.
Did you know you needed a heart transplant?
When the roll is called up yonder, will you be there?
You need Jesus.
Can I just share that . . .

Instead of feeling inspired, Christy felt frustrated.

Witnessing shouldn't be this hard! What's my problem? The most important thing in the world is whether a person understands how to be saved and have eternal life through Christ. Why can't I figure out a way to say that so it sounds natural?

When she arrived home from work that night, the two cards and the booklets were still in her purse, untouched.

But before she went to bed, a page of flowery stationery was folded in half and slipped into the back of her Bible. At the top of the page appeared, "Christy's Hit List." Two names were written below.

Chapter 7

The Little Mouse

The next two weeks were filled with homework, ski club meetings, Wednesday night Bible study, and Christy's usual Friday night and Saturday hours at the pet store. The blank cards and unused booklets remained in her purse.

"Do you think I'll raise all the money in time?" Katie asked Christy as they walked down the school halls after their ski club meeting. "We're leaving in ten days, and how much more did they say I needed? Thirty dollars?"

"Must be, because we've sold about five boxes of the candy bars at the pet store. Jon bought a box, and then your first box you basically paid for. I think Mr. Riley said you needed thirty-two dollars more."

"I can get that by next Monday, right?" Katie said, looking hopeful. "I'm baby-sitting on Thursday night, and if more candy bars sell this week at the pet store, I should be able to come up with the thirty-two dollars, right?"

"I'm sure it'll work out," Christy said as they paused in the school parking lot in front of Katie's car.

"How much homework do you have?"

"Not much. A chapter to read for government and a dialogue to memorize for Spanish."

"Do you want to come over to my house, and we could do our homework together?" Christy offered.

"I probably should get home so I can, well, you know, work on my Spanish." Katie's expression lit up. "Did I tell you I got an A on my last Spanish test?"

"Could it be the result of a certain Spanish tutor from Ecuador?" Christy teased.

She felt happy for Katie's budding friendship with Glen. He definitely had found a place in her life.

It all started when Katie bravely called Glen one night a few days after the Pizza Feed to ask a question about the pronunciation of a word in her Spanish dialogue. Glen not only gave her the answer, but he also talked with her for more than two hours.

The next Sunday he remained timid around Katie. Christy thought he seemed shy and unsure of himself. But the day after that, Glen called Katie, and they talked for another two hours.

Their relationship seemed a little peculiar to Christy. Katie, however, appeared content with how things were progressing, and Christy thought it best to stay out of it.

"I probably should get going," Katie said. "I told Glen I'd call him if I got stuck with my Spanish, and it looks like I'll need to call him early. Our last conversation went until after ten-thirty, and my mom said I shouldn't be on the phone that long." Katie smiled brightly and said, "See you tomorrow. Happy homework!"

Yeah, happy homework all by myself.

A barrage of weird thoughts bombarded Christy. Now she sort of knew how Katie felt when Christy was dating Rick. It was a strange, almost competitive, feeling, as if she should be mad at Glen for taking Katie away from her. She hadn't expected to feel this way, and she hadn't ever expected Katie to be so preoccupied with anything or anyone else that she would put off Christy this way.

Christy drove home, went right inside, and pulled a jacket from her closet. "I'm going for a walk around the block before I start my homework," she explained to her mom.

"Are you okay?" Mom asked.

"I'm fine. I've been sitting all day, and I need to get some oxygen to my brain before I tackle the books."

"Well, be careful."

"I'm only going around the block."

"The wind has kicked up, and it's chilly out. Did you get a jacket?"

"Yes," Christy called out as she pulled the front door shut and let the screen door slam in the wind.

A few crinkled, brown leaves skipped across the yard, and the air had a bit of a nip to it. It was good thinking weather.

She walked briskly and contemplated the ski trip,

only a week and a half away. It looked as though she was really going, with no turning back now. Christy told herself it would be fun and a good experience. A little part of her felt the disappointment she had seen on her mom's face when Mom realized this was the first time their family wouldn't be together for Thanksgiving.

Instead of turkey, stuffing, and cranberries next Thursday, Christy figured she would be eating corn dogs and cocoa. It certainly wasn't enough of a reason for her to back out of her promise to Katie. Nevertheless, the realization made her sad.

The only good part about being gone over Thanksgiving was that since Rick would probably be home, she wouldn't have to see him or talk things through with him. Deep down she knew she did the right thing by breaking up with him. It was disappointing, though, that their relationship had turned into an "all or nothing" one. She would have liked to have been friends with him. Even better friends than they had been during last school year.

The change in her relationship with Katie disappointed her too. Christy knew it was crazy to be jealous of Glen, yet she recognized the feeling, and at least to herself, she admitted that was exactly what she felt.

It'd be different if I had a boyfriend now too. Or at least someone I was going out with occasionally. I wonder if Katie and I will ever have boyfriends at the same time. I wonder if we'll ever double-date.

The thoughts she had pushed down for the last few weeks began to stir up to the top as she turned the corner and headed up the block, back to her house. The wind was now in her face, and she pushed into it, pushing her heart's feelings to the surface at the same time.

I wonder when I'll see Todd again. Will things be like they were, or have both of us changed so much we can never go back to how it was? I wonder if he received my card. I wonder if he liked it. I wonder if I should write him again or wait until he writes me back.

She lowered her head and pushed forward. The oncoming wind made her eyes water, and aloud she told herself, "Why do you think he'd write you? He never has written you before. Todd is Todd, and his life doesn't include you right now. It might someday. And then again, it might not. You have to go on, Christy."

She walked up the steps to her front porch and righted a terra-cotta planter that the wind had knocked over. It reminded her of the first time they had seen this house. The screen on the door had been torn, and a smashed clay pot had lain scattered across the porch. That was only a little more than a year ago. One year, and so much had changed in her life.

Why do things have to change? Why can't anything stay the same—just for a little while? Why does God blow His reckless, raging wind through my life and scatter everything and everyone around?

She tugged open the front door. As soon as she

entered the warm house, Christy was aware of her wind-buffeted cheeks turning rosy and of the wonderful, strong smell of Mom's meat loaf and baked potatoes in the oven.

Even though it was still a week and a half before Thanksgiving, the day when people were supposed to think of all they were grateful for, Christy decided to do a preliminary rundown. She headed straight for her room, took off her jacket, plopped on her bed, and began a list in her diary.

"I'm thankful for my parents, this house, my health, and all the blessings God has given us, like food and clothes. I'm thankful for my friends and . . ."

Christy paused. The thought had come so quickly, she wasn't sure if she should write it. She decided to go with the flow and wrote, ". . . I'm thankful for Todd. And Rick. And Katie. And for my job, my church, my relationship with Jesus, and the way I can talk with Him anytime and anywhere."

Then, because it somehow ended up sounding like a prayer, Christy wrote "Amen" at the bottom of the page.

Wednesday night Luke had the high school Bible study do almost the same thing. He passed out paper and pens and had everyone think of something they were thankful for that they had never consciously thanked God for. Then they were to write Him a letter, thanking Him for whatever it was.

Christy thought hard and finally wrote, "God, I'm thankful for my eyesight. I've always taken it for granted. I'm thankful I can see."

Luke gave everyone another piece of paper and told them to think of someone they were thankful for and to write a note to that person, explaining why they were thankful.

Christy thought at first she should write her note to Katie. Sneaking a peek at Katie's letter, she noticed Katie had gone right to work, writing Glen a thank-you note for his help in Spanish. Somehow she lost her zeal to write to Katie.

In the end, Christy wrote hers to her parents, thanking them for all they had done for her.

Even though she and Katie were sitting together for the whole Bible study, it seemed as if Katie barely noticed Christy. As soon as the study ended, Katie sprang from her chair like a panther.

Christy watched as Katie slipped between the haphazard rows of folding chairs before striking up a conversation with Glen. He seemed to enjoy the attention.

The minute Katie handed him the thank-you note, Glen's face turned a little red. He stuck the note in his pocket without reading it. Then he stood there, face still a bit rosy, while Katie talked on, using her nonstop hand motions to demonstrate everything she was saying to him.

Even though Christy felt some twinges of jealousy over Katie's attention to Glen, she couldn't help but feel happy for Katie. Glen seemed to benefit from their friendship, and Katie definitely was too.

Christy drove home thinking about how much fun they were going to have on the ski trip. At the same time, she felt guilty for thinking it. She knew that one of the reasons they were going to have so much fun was because neither of them was interested in any of the guys who were going.

Now if Glen were going on the trip, Christy probably would have decided to stay home. She wasn't sure if that was immature or not, but she was sure she and Katie would have a lot more fun without any boyfriend problems for the weekend.

When Christy arrived home, Mom had already gone to bed, but Dad was watching TV in the recliner. Christy handed him the note and waited for his reaction.

Her dad read the thank-you. Then he pulled the side lever on the recliner, expecting the footrest to pop up. Instead, the backrest reclined, almost all the way to the floor. For a minute, it looked as though Dad might be hurled over the back of the chair.

Christy jumped over to his side, prepared to try to block the launch. But her dad had managed to balance the recliner, with no damage done to the space capsule or the astronaut.

"Well," he said, chuckling, "thanks for the note of encouragement. With all the things I do wrong around here, it's nice to know somebody thinks I do a few things right!"

He patted the side of the recliner for emphasis, and

Christy remembered his dismantling and "fixing" it a few weeks ago.

She hugged him around the neck and said, "You do a lot of things right. I don't always remember to thank you, but I should."

"You know," Dad said solemnly, "your mother and I are letting you go on this ski trip, but neither of us feels too comfortable with the whole thing."

"Why?"

"You've never skied before, you're going with a bunch of people we don't know, and as far as we know, you and Katie are the only Christians. We just don't feel certain it's the best thing you could be doing."

Christy panicked. "Are you saying I can't go?"

"No. We've discussed it, and you're so sure about it, we agreed you should go. Your mother and I don't feel comfortable with it, that's all."

Christy wasn't sure how to respond. Were her parents hinting she should withdraw from the trip on her own? Were they sending her but withholding their blessing? Were they really leaving the choice up to her? What should she say?

"I don't think the school would let us take a trip like this if anything bad had ever happened," she ventured. "Mr. Riley is the sponsor, and he said he and his wife have taken the club every year for the past four years. I'm sure I'll be okay."

"I suppose you will. You've been on greater adventures than this, no doubt. I just wanted you to know I have some reservations."

Dad pushed himself out of the recliner and, turning off the TV, said, "Well, that's all I wanted to say. Thanks for the note."

Christy followed him down the hall, remembering when she was a little girl on their Wisconsin farm. One of her favorite pastimes had been to follow her dad around in the barn. He was so big she could easily hide behind him. If she walked softly in the hay, he wouldn't even know she was there.

Sometimes his long strides would suddenly come to a halt, and she would bump into him. Then he would scoop her into his arms, lift her over his head, and bellow for the cows to hear, "Look, I've found a little mouse! Listen to her squeal."

He would say that, because by then Christy would be giggling, squealing, and pleading to be put down.

Following her dad down the hall tonight, she realized she was now only six inches shorter than he. At sixteen years old, she would never be scooped up in his arms again to be held over his head and called his little mouse. She was almost a woman, and he was almost treating her like one.

On impulse, right before Dad opened the bedroom door, Christy spoke. "Dad?"

He turned to face her, but she wasn't sure what she wanted to say. Instead of trying to find the words, Christy wrapped her arms around him and pressed her cheek into his shoulder.

Dad returned the hug. They looked at each other
and smiled. Christy was certain he knew exactly what
she had been thinking.

He brushed back her long bangs with his rough
hand, kissed her on the forehead, and said, "Good
night, my little mouse."

Chapter 8

96817

Make sure you've turned in your medical release, otherwise we'll leave you in the school parking lot on Wednesday. Nobody goes without a signed medical release form!" Mr. Riley made his announcement loud and clear as the ski club was breaking up after its final meeting before the trip.

"And don't forget you're each responsible for your meals on the way up and back. Did I leave anything out? Oh, right, your luggage." Mr. Riley raised his voice. "Everyone, listen! Bring your luggage to school on Wednesday morning and take it to the teachers' lounge. One bag each, one sleeping bag, and one carryon, like a small backpack, that you'll keep with you in the van. Okay, any questions?"

"Yeah," one of the guys asked from his perch on top of Mr. Riley's desk, "is there any snow?"

"I heard a storm's coming in tonight. Let's hope it dumps a ton on the mountains for the next two days and that it clears up by the time we hit the slopes on Thursday."

"I hope we don't have to drive through the snow,"

Christy confided to Katie. "Our family got stuck in a blizzard once when I was seven, and we had to spend the night in our car."

"Really?" Katie asked. "How scary! I've never even seen snow."

"What?" Christy asked, stopping Katie in her tracks. "How could you live to be sixteen years old and never see snow?"

"I've lived in southern California all my life, and my family doesn't travel much. That's why I've always wanted to go skiing."

Christy said, "I can't believe this, Katie. Do you have any idea how cold and wet and miserable snow can be? Do you have any idea how hard it is to walk in it or keep your balance on an icy sidewalk?"

"Nope," Katie said honestly.

"This is going to be quite a trip; I can tell already. Are you sure you have enough warm clothes? And did you get your money all straightened out?"

"My parents gave me the last twenty dollars I needed, and whatever we get from the candy bars you still have at the pet store will be my meal money for the trip."

"I'm stopping by there on the way home. Jon's so nice, he's even giving me my paycheck early so I'll have extra spending money."

"Just think," Katie said, "you were planning on using all those paychecks to buy back your bracelet."

"I know. I still have no idea who paid it off," Christy said, rubbing her thumb over the thin gold band. "Anyway, I'll get the rest of your candy money and give it to you tomorrow."

Christy hoped the remainder of the candy bars had sold. On Saturday she had noticed at least a box and a half left.

When she entered the pet store that afternoon, Jon was standing by the register, swatting the air with a small goldfish net.

"What are you doing?" Christy asked, "Trying to catch a flying fish?"

"Very funny. No, I'm trying to catch a fly. I like feeding my lizards the old-fashioned, organic way. Whoa!" Jon swooped the net through the air inches from Christy's face, and then squeezed the opening closed with his fingers.

Christy peered at the goldfish net he held before her. Sure enough, he had caught a fly.

"Can you watch the register while I take this to the lizards?" Jon asked as he walked away. Then turning around, he said, "Wait a minute! You're not working today, are you?"

"No. I came in to pick up the candy bars and . . ." She let her sentence trail off, deciding it might be rude to assume Jon was still planning to give her paycheck to her early.

"That's right. I almost forgot. Could you watch the register anyway? I'll be right back."

For some reason, Christy felt funny walking behind the counter and standing by the register when it wasn't her day to work. Almost like she was sneaking into a place she didn't belong.

Just then a man who had been in the back of the store came up to the register with a large bag in his arms. He looked slightly familiar, but Christy wasn't sure where she had seen him before.

He dropped the bag onto the counter with a thump and said, "Glad to see you finally got someone around here who knows how to order your stuff for you."

The label on the bag said, "Birdseed." Then Christy remembered when she had seen this man before.

Without letting on that she recognized him, she quickly rang up the sale and hoped he would leave quietly without causing a scene like last time.

"Two dollars for a candy bar?" the man bellowed when he read the sign on the box. "What kind of highway robbery is that? And what kind of a pet store sells food for humans? There's probably some city ordinance against that. What kind of city would let some jerk sell food for humans and food for animals over the same counter?"

"Here's your change, sir," Christy said, her hand shaking.

He snatched the three one-dollar bills from her and, grappling with his bag of birdseed, stormed off.

"Another satisfied customer, I see," Jon said, coming up to the front.

"What's with that guy? And by the way, thanks for letting me be the lucky one to wait on him." Christy slung her purse over her shoulder and stepped away from the register, indicating she was now off duty.

"Aw, don't let him bother you. He likes being miserable. He's in here at least once a week, and he always finds something to gripe about. What was it this time?"

"The candy bars. But that's okay, because I'm taking them, and he won't be able to call the city officials and have them fine you for selling dog food and chocolate over the same counter." Christy did a quick count of the bars left in the box and asked, "Are there any more in back?"

"That's the last of them," Jon said, reaching in his pocket. "My sister called and said they were good, so here." He stuck a wad of money in Christy's hand. "I'll buy the rest of them."

"You don't have to do that," Christy protested. Uncrumpling the bill in her hand and realizing it was a twenty, she said, "This is too much. There are only three candy bars left. That's six dollars, not twenty."

"Keep the change," Jon said. "Buy yourself a snow cone or something this weekend. Buy one for your friend too. What's her name? Katie?"

"Yeah, Katie. Thanks, Jon. This is really generous of you."

Jon reached into the box and pulled out the three last candy bars. "Here," he said, tossing one to Christy. "Have a candy bar. And here." He tossed her another one. "Give this one to Katie."

Then he unwrapped the third bar and bit into it. "Your

paycheck and the envelope with the candy money are in the cash register. Let me get it for you."

Christy decided to join Jon in devouring the final candy bars. She unwrapped one he had tossed her and discovered it had almonds. She hated nuts. Then she remembered how she had tried macadamia nuts on her frozen yogurt when she was in Maui. She liked the macadamia nuts. Maybe she would like these almonds.

The first bite she let melt slowly in her mouth until all that was left was the almond. Then, with a crunch, she chewed it up and swallowed.

"Here you go," Jon said, handing Christy the two envelopes. "Have a great time, don't break any bones, and see you back here at work next Friday."

"Thanks again," Christy said, taking another bite of the chocolate-and-almond experiment. She decided her dislike of nuts must have been a childhood thing. To her sixteen-year-old palate, there was nothing about nuts to dislike.

"Oh, before you go, I wanted to ask you something," Jon said. "What church do you go to?"

Christy couldn't believe he was asking her. This might be the opportunity to witness she had been praying for. She quickly swallowed the chunk of chocolate and almonds.

After she told Jon the name of her church, she watched as he pulled out a piece of paper and a pen.

"How do you get there?" he asked, carefully writing down the directions.

"And what time does church start?"

Christy gave him all the information; then, because her curiosity was killing her, she asked, "Why? I mean, how did you know I was a Christian?"

"When you applied for this job," Jon stated, "you wrote on the application you wouldn't work on Sundays, so I figured you went to church somewhere. Then I've been watching you to see if you lived all those things they teach in church about being honest and not stealing and all that."

Christy's eyebrows went up as she waited for him to finish.

"So far, so good. I like what I see."

This is too good to be true! God is answering my prayer about witnessing to Jon. And I haven't even said anything!

Feeling excited and a bit proud of her strong Christian example, Christy said, "So you're saying that because you see Jesus in me, you're interested in going to church?"

"No," Jon answered.

Christy tried not to let the disappointment and puzzlement show on her face.

"I asked about church because I have an old friend from college who's coming to stay with me over Thanksgiving. He's one of those 'born-agains,' and I know he's going to want to go to a church around here on Sunday, if not on Thanksgiving. You're the only one I know who goes to church."

Then, because she didn't want this witnessing opportunity to die such a humiliating death, Christy mustered her courage and said, "Why don't you go with him, Jon? I think you'd like my church."

A slight smile crept across Jon's face. "You've got me targeted now, don't you? I guess I don't mind a little nudge toward heaven every now and then. Just promise me you won't be like one girl who used to work here. She never said a word about being born again or anything. She just left these little . . . what are they called? Tracts? Well, she left them everywhere around the store, only she did it in secret. Guess she thought nobody would figure out who they were from."

Jon shook his head, still grinning. "We used to call her the Easter Bunny."

Christy breathed a sigh of relief that she hadn't tried the same technique with her cards and booklets.

"I say, if you're going to believe something, then believe it enough to take a stand and not be sneaky about it," Jon said, looking directly at Christy.

Words bubbled up in Christy's heart and tumbled out of her mouth before she had a chance to critique them. "I believe you need to turn your life over to God."

"Oh, you do?" Now Jon was laughing.

Christy knew him well enough to realize he was genuinely amused.

"Well, now, I like that, Christy. You believe something strongly enough to say it. I admire you for that. You might try a little tact with your honesty. But I wouldn't be surprised if you told me you're praying for me."

Christy's boldness began to evaporate, and she could feel her cheeks flushing under Jon's intense gaze. In a much smaller voice, she said, "As a matter of fact, I have been praying for you."

Now Jon was surprised. "I guess it can't hurt," he said, slipping behind the counter to help a customer who was approaching the cash register.

"Have a great weekend," Jon said as he smiled his good-bye.

The next day at lunch, Christy delivered to Katie the money from Jon along with a rundown on her witnessing opportunity.

"Can you imagine what would have happened if you had given him that card and tract?" Katie asked.

"I know. Makes me think how much easier my life would be if I wouldn't try to run ahead of God," Christy said, sticking her hand into her lunch bag.

"Oh, look what I have for you!" she said, presenting Katie with the candy bar. "A gift from Jon."

"Looks like you and I are going on a ski trip tomorrow!" Katie said excitedly. "Let's celebrate. I'll share the final candy bar with you to salute our victory over the near-fiasco fund-raiser."

Katie broke the bar in two, handed the larger piece to Christy, and then held up her half. "Here's to the best friend anyone could ever have—Christy Miller! I couldn't have made it without you, Chris."

"Sure you could have," Christy said. "I wouldn't have made it without Aunt Marti. I never thought I'd say this, but here's to Aunt Marti."

The two girls chomped into their chocolate at the same time.

"So, are you beginning to feel those chemicals affecting your brain yet?" Christy asked as soon as she swallowed the first bite.

Katie blushed and said, "He called me again last night. I'm kind of sorry we're not going to be around for Bible study or church. I think Glen might be getting a little more confident. After all these long talks on the phone, he's bound to sit by me at church pretty soon, don't you think?"

"Well, if you feel that strongly about seeing him, we could back out of the ski trip," Christy ventured.

"Are you kidding? After all we've been through with the fund-raiser and everything? No way! We're committed to this trip, Christy." Katie added with a twinkle, "Glen will just have to wait for me to return, because I'm the kind of girl who is worth waiting for."

"You are, Katie. And don't you ever forget it!"

Christy began to pack for the trip the minute she arrived home from school. It seemed to take forever. She rolled the ski clothes because they fit better in her bag that way. The tough part was deciding what else to bring. She started with two pairs of sweats, but they were too bulky. She managed to narrow it down to one pair of sweat pants and two sweat shirts. The turtlenecks and T-shirts fit easily. The choice of sweaters became tricky, and in the end, she only took one and decided to wear the other one to school tomorrow.

"How's it coming?" Mom asked, popping her head into Christy's room.

"I think I have it all stuffed in," Christy said, wrestling with the big black zipper on top of the bag.

"Did you include some tights? And how about your mittens?"

Christy let the zipper go and flopped backward on the floor. "No," she moaned. "I forgot all my underwear too."

"Looks like you need a bigger bag," Mom said with a chuckle.

"We're only allowed to bring one."

"I think there's one in the garage that's a little bigger than that one. I'll be right back."

Mom returned with an old, green, beat-up Army duffel bag that was definitely bigger than the newer, slick, black one Christy had been cramming her stuff into.

"Mom, that old thing is falling apart, and it's totally ugly. I wouldn't want to be caught dead carrying that thing."

Even though Mom looked as though she was about to correct Christy, she only dropped the green bag on the floor and said, "Then you work it out. Dinner will be ready in fifteen minutes."

Now Christy sat alone on her bedroom floor, half of her wanting to pout like a little girl and the other half demanding she act like an independent young woman packing for a ski trip. It was up to her to decide if she wanted to take everything she needed and be seen with the dorky-looking bag or take fewer clothes in the cool-looking bag.

Dumping everything out on the floor, she reevaluated what she actually needed and what she could leave behind. She needed everything, and more. It looked like the dorky bag was the only way to go. How disgusting and how humiliating. It even smelled gross.

As they were finishing dinner, Mom casually asked if Christy had managed to work out her packing situation.

"Yeah," Christy mumbled into her forkful of peas, "I'm taking the green bag."

"I think you'll be glad you did," Mom said, standing and beginning to clear the table. "Oh, by the way, this came in the mail today for you. Any idea what it is?"

Mom picked up a small slip of paper off the cluttered part of the counter and handed it to Christy. It was a notice from the post office indicating it was holding a package for Christy Miller with postage due. It didn't state who the package was from.

"I don't know," Christy said, turning the slip over and examining the back. "All it says is fifty-seven cents are due on a package."

"Let me see it. Who's it from?" David asked.

"I don't know. I haven't ordered anything lately. I have all the ski stuff Aunt Marti was sending."

"It should have the zip code it was sent from on it,"

Dad said, putting out his hand. "Can I have a look?"

Christy handed him the slip, and Dad said, "It was sent from 96817. Has to be somewhere on the West Coast. I thought maybe your grandmother had sent something, but her zip wouldn't start with a nine."

"Can you pick it up for me tomorrow?" Christy asked. "I'm leaving right after school for the ski trip, so I won't be able to get to the post office until Monday."

"Sure. Leave it where I'll see it," Mom said.

I wonder who sent me a package. What could it possibly be?

Chapter 9

The Inside-Outsider

Paying attention in class proved to be nearly impossible by fifth period Wednesday afternoon. The teachers were already in vacation mode, and the students, whether they had weekend plans or not, were talking about anything and everything but class work.

When the final bell rang, Christy hurried to the teachers' lounge and found Katie already there, digging her luggage out of the heap.

"I have your bag, Christy. It's over there by the couch. Do you have your carryon and your jacket?"

"My jacket is still in my locker. I'm going to run to get it and put these books back. Do you need anything from your locker?" Christy asked.

"I'm all set. I'll wait here for you."

Christy bustled her way through the loud, crowded hallway, surprised that her heart was beating so hard and fast.

I guess I thought this day would never come. I thought something would happen, and we'd never actually go on the trip. But now it's here, and I'm going—green bag and all. So I'd better make the best of it and stop being a chicken.

She spun through the combination on her lock, grabbed her jacket, crammed in her books, and met Katie back in the teachers' lounge, all in about five minutes.

Katie had on her backpack, her jacket was tied around her waist, her duffel bag was slung over her shoulder, and her sleeping bag was tucked under her arm. "Mr. Riley said to carry our stuff out to the van in the parking lot. Are you ready?"

"I think so." Christy grabbed her bulky duffel bag and looped her carryon over her shoulder. With the other hand she snatched her sleeping bag and jacket.

"No offense," Katie said, eyeing the drab-olive monster bag, "but didn't you have any other suitcases or anything? You look like you're going to boot camp."

Christy did take offense at the comment. Not because it was Katie who said it, but because she had almost convinced herself the duffel bag was not a big deal and that no one would even notice it. To have Katie comment on it meant all her fears of being rejected by the entire ski club were, in fact, well-founded.

"Let's just go," Christy said, pushing past Katie to the door. Maybe, if they hurried, Mr. Riley would load their stuff first, and no one else would notice her bag.

But by the time they arrived at the van, they were the last to deliver their bags. To Christy's chagrin, her bag was placed on top of the heap. The van door was slammed shut, and her bag was the only one showing. In fact, it took up the whole back window.

The worst part was that her dad had decided last night to mark the bag for her, as if someone else would happen to bring a matching bag. With a black permanent marker he had written "MILLER" in huge letters across the side. Of course, that was the side facing out. Not only would the whole school know that Christy Miller belonged to that ugly green bag, but all who drove past them from here to Lake Tahoe would also know.

Everyone else had already claimed their seats inside the van. Christy and Katie found two tight-squeeze spots left in the front bench seat, right behind the driver. Definitely not the cool place to sit.

Christy slid in first, next to the window, feeling as though everyone was watching her. It was one thing to show up at a meeting for the ski club with these people scattered around a classroom. There it didn't matter that no one knew her name or paid attention to her. But it felt completely different to be jammed in a van with these same people and to know they would be together in tight quarters for the next four days.

Feeling hot from embarrassment and from the warm ski sweater she was wearing, Christy tried to open the window next to her. She pushed and pinched but couldn't figure it out.

Katie leaned over and released the catch in an

instant. The window slid open easily. With a laugh and in a loud voice, Katie said, "You have to be smarter than the window, Miller."

Christy bored her eyes into her sudden traitor-friend and kept shooting visual darts until Katie caught on that her comment had hurt. It was bad enough that the slam had been inflicted in front of all these strangers, but Christy wondered why Katie suddenly called her "Miller." Was it so they would all know she was the Miller who went with the green monster bag?

"Hey, it was only a joke," Katie said. "Take a chill pill, Christy. You're not wigging out on me, are you?"

What are you doing, Katie? What's with this slang all of a sudden? Are you trying to show these people you're cool, and I'm not?

Just then Mr. Riley climbed into the driver's seat, and his blond, athletic-looking wife joined him in the front passenger seat.

"Hey, Don, I need your medical release form," Mr. Riley yelled to the back of the van.

"Oh, man!" Don rose from his prime spot and said, "It's in my locker. I'll be right back."

"Hustle, Donald!" Mr. Riley called after him. "It's not fair for you to keep the rest of the group waiting."

Mrs. Riley turned around and introduced herself to Katie and Christy. "You girls can call me Janet this weekend. I know Lou still wants everyone to call him Mr. Riley, but I prefer you call me Janet."

She seemed sweet, and Christy felt a little relieved

that their woman leader was so approachable.

"Have you girls ever been to Tahoe before? It's so beautiful up there."

For some reason Christy added, "Katie's never even seen snow before." It sounded like a jab, and Christy realized she must have said it to get back at Katie for the earlier slams she had made on Christy.

But the remark didn't faze Katie a bit. She unashamedly admitted she had never seen snow and began to draw all kinds of ski advice out of Janet.

Don returned with the medical form, Mr. Riley started up the van, and soon they were on their way. For the first forty-five minutes or so, Christy looked out the window and listened to Katie ramble on with Janet and Mr. Riley as if they were old friends. The guy sitting on the other side of Katie had turned around in his seat and was involved in a conversation with the girl right behind him. The rest of the group settled into their conversations and natural groupings.

The three cool guys had taken over the back of the van. They were all popular, and Don seemed to be the leader of the three. They already had on their skier sunglasses and were stretched out on the backseat, talking loudly about moguls and how much air they had caught on certain ski runs at Squaw. Don said that one year there was so much snow he had skied at Squaw on the Fourth of July. No one questioned him or his skiing expertise. Don and the other guys brought their own skis and poles. Their collection of expensive equipment was tied down on top of the van.

In front of the guys were the rich girls. There were three of them too, and they all wore their hair the same way—shoulder-length, permed, and color-treated with blond highlights. They all had straight white teeth and perfectly clear skin. Christy didn't know any of their names, but her guess was they probably all had the same name too.

In the middle was a couple and a girl named Julie, who looked as though she was about to become part of another couple with the guy sitting next to Katie.

It didn't take a genius to figure out that Katie and Christy were the leftovers. Funny how a person could be part of the "in" group and still feel like an outsider.

They drove for hours, and Christy slept a good part of the way. Her jacket worked as the perfect pillow against the closed van window. She regretted coming on the trip. With Katie treating her the way she had, Christy did not look forward to the thought of four more days of the same.

It was dark when they stopped for dinner. Christy stumbled out of the van and saw that they were at Jacque's Cafe, a little restaurant in an even littler town. Someone asked why they hadn't gone on to Bishop for dinner.

"This is our traditional stopping place," said Mr. Riley. "They have great food, and I always like giving Jacque the business. Go on in, guys."

The group filed in and waited to be seated. The

hostess showed them to three large booths. Everyone
scrambled to find a place. Katie scooted in right next to
Janet in the booth with Mr. Riley and the three popular
guys. Before Christy could wedge in, all the places
were filled.

The booth next to them held the two couples, and
she wasn't about to interfere with that foursome. All
that was left was a spot with the three rich girls.

"Can I squeeze in here?" Christy asked the girl on the
end, expecting rejection or at least a disdainful look.

To her surprise, the girl said, "Sure, Christy."

Scooting over, she introduced Christy to the other
girls. "I'm Shannon," the girl said. "And that's Jennifer
and Tiffany."

Christy was surprised at their sudden friendliness.
At the same time she felt suspicious of their willing-
ness to accept her into their group.

"You know," Shannon said, handing Christy a
menu, "I've been wanting to tell you this for a long
time, and I guess this is the perfect opportunity."

Now Christy was really surprised Not only did this
girl know her name, but she also had something she
wanted to tell Christy.

"I thought what you did last year at the final assembly when you gave up your cheerleading spot to Teri
Moreno was a really awesome thing," Shannon said.
"I've always wanted to tell you that, but I didn't know
you or anything, and you're always hanging out with
that other girl who used to be a mascot."

Jennifer and Tiffany snickered behind their menus. One of them mumbled, "If you're not coordinated enough to be a cheerleader, I guess the next best thing is a mascot."

"That way you can hide in a cougar costume, and when you fall all over the football field, everyone thinks you're doing it on purpose."

Christy didn't join in their giggling. She opened her menu and looked down for a long time, trying to sort this out. It hurt her that these girls were making fun of Katie, yet at the moment she was still miffed at Katie. The amazing thing was that these girls had noticed her and accepted her into their group.

Maybe this is going to be a missions trip, like Katie said. If these girls are willing to let me be friends with them, maybe they'll let me tell them about the Lord. This could be a God-thing. If only Katie would support me a little here.

When the waitress came, all three girls ordered the chicken club sandwich. Christy was the last to order. She had planned on having a hamburger and french fries but at the last minute told the waitress, "I'll have the same thing."

"Mayo on the side, like the others?" the waitress asked.

"Sure, that would be fine."

The girls all smiled at Christy, and she felt as if she had passed some sort of secret initiation. Was it the mayo on the side or the chicken club?

Chicken club, Christy thought. *If that doesn't perfectly describe me, I don't know what does!*

The three girls included Christy in their conversation during the meal and gave her all kinds of pointers on skiing. They had learned to ski when they were little kids and seemed quite experienced, yet they weren't snooty about it. They told Christy over and over that she would have a great time.

By the end of their meal, Christy was beginning to believe them.

Chapter 10

Up Close and Personal

The van pulled up in front of a condominium complex somewhere on the North Shore of Lake Tahoe well after midnight.

"Okay, everyone," Mr. Riley said, turning off the engine and turning on the lights inside the van. "We have numbers four and five. Let's put all the girls in number four and the guys in number five. Grab your own stuff, and then you guys come back to help me with the ice chests on the roof."

Christy, still squinting from the sudden bright light, climbed out of the van and stumbled on the gravel driveway to the back. The first thing she noticed was the white blanket of snow covering the ground in front of the condo. The parking area and walkways had been cleared, but everything else under the streetlight's beacon looked as though it had been spread with white frosting.

"Snow!" Katie cheered. "Look, there's snow!" She scooped up a handful and playfully tossed the loose powder into the air.

"Wheee!" she squealed, pressing together a snowball.

The three girls stood beside Christy at the back of the van, and one of them asked, "What's with her?"

"She's never seen snow before."

"In her life?"

"No, this is the first time."

The girls gave each other knowing looks, and Christy realized what they were thinking. Katie wasn't rich like they were. She didn't travel and wear designer clothes like they did. She clearly wasn't "one of them."

Christy wasn't sure why they accepted her, though. Was it just the cheerleader thing or something else?

Christy pulled on her jacket and was aware of the cold creeping through her tennis shoes and socks. It was a familiar, Wisconsin-winter feeling, and one she hadn't missed since they had moved to California. She hated having cold feet.

Don started handing out luggage, and since Christy's bag was the first to come out, she thought, *If these girls think I'm their caliber, this duffel bag ought to set them straight right away.*

"Is that your bag?" Tiffany asked, sounding surprised.

Oh, oh, here it comes. Oh, well. The popularity was nice while it lasted.

"Yes," Christy admitted, "it's mine."

"Where did you get it?" Tiffany asked, touching it as if to test its authenticity. "I looked at Goodwill,

Salvation Army, and the Army-Navy Surplus, and they didn't have any more."

Christy thought Tiffany was mocking her and was about to get upset when she noticed that the other two girls were looking at her bag with the same admiration. Not one of them was smirking.

"I . . . I got it out of our garage. It was my dad's. I don't know where he got it."

"You are so lucky," Tiffany said sincerely. "All I could find was a pair of Army boots. My mom had them resoled and waterproofed for this trip. They're in my bag; I'll show them to you when we get inside. You're going to bunk with us, aren't you?"

Christy couldn't believe it. These girls were serious. Apparently old Army gear was "in," and she didn't even know it. Why else would a rich girl, who could buy any pair of boots in the mall, hunt down an old pair in the thrift stores and have them fixed up? Christy had a lot to learn about this group of girls.

Janet led the seven girls into the two-story condo and flipped on the lights. It was much more spacious than Christy had expected. There were three bedrooms and three bathrooms, and an upstairs living room and kitchen that looked out on the lake.

"This is huge!" Katie exclaimed. "Where do you want us, Janet?"

"If you girls don't mind, I'd like to take the little bedroom upstairs. It only has a double bed in it. These two downstairs bedrooms have four beds in each, so there's plenty of room for you."

"Let's take this one," Katie said, preparing to dump her bag in the nearest bedroom.

"This room is already taken," Tiffany said. Jennifer and Shannon slid past Tiffany and tossed their bags on the floor to visually back up Tiffany's statement.

"Fine, we'll go in the other room," Katie said, heading down the hallway. "Come on, Christy."

Christy felt torn. She had made inroads with the three rich girls, and there was an extra bed in with them. They had invited her to stay with them. It was the perfect witnessing opportunity. And yet, after all, the reason she had agreed to come on this trip was to be a support to Katie.

"I'd better go in the other room," Christy said quietly to the three girls. "Katie and I kind of planned this trip together, you know."

"Well, if you change your mind, you're welcome in our room anytime," Shannon said.

Christy started to lug her stuff down the hall.

"Hey," Tiffany called out after her, "as soon as you unload your stuff, come down, and I'll show you my boots."

"Okay," Christy agreed. Somehow she felt like a traitor, yet it was hard to tell which side she was betraying.

"Look!" Katie exclaimed as Christy entered the room. "Daybeds! Do you want to be on top or on the pullout?"

"Doesn't matter to me. Which do you want?"

The other two girls entered the room, their boyfriends carrying their luggage. They said "Hi," dumped their stuff, and left with the guys.

"Guess we won't be seeing much of them this weekend," Katie said. "I'll take the bottom bed. You can have the top."

"I don't mind the bottom," Christy said. "Besides, the bottom pops up if you want to be up higher."

"No, this is fine. I don't mind, really."

"Christy," came a call from down the hallway. "Are you coming?"

Katie gave Christy a questioning look.

"Tiffany has a pair of boots she wants to show me," Christy explained.

"Oh, well, then let's go." Katie led the way down the hall as if she had been invited as well.

I have a horrible feeling about this!

"Katie," Christy said, latching onto Katie's shoulder and pulling her back toward their room. "Remember how you said a few weeks ago at Bible study that this trip was like our missions trip?" She spoke in a soft voice and hoped Katie would be open to what she was trying to convey.

"Oh," Katie said, nodding her head. "Right! You think these three might be the ones we've been sent to witness to."

"Something like that," Christy said, keeping her voice low. "I think we should try to be open in case we experience some, you know, like hostility, or something. Don't take it personally."

"Good point," Katie agreed. "I know these girls, and they can be really snooty. I'm glad you recognize that about them, because I'd hate for you to get your feelings hurt the first night."

My feelings, Katie! I'm trying to protect your feelings here.

Katie had already begun to march down the hall like a crusader. All Christy could do was follow. As she expected, when they approached the room, all three girls gave Katie a what-are-you-doing-here look. Katie seemed oblivious.

"Are those your boots?" Christy asked quickly, hoping to divert the girls' attention away from Katie. She bent down and picked up one of the clunky-looking fossils. "Do these really fit you?"

"They're a little big. Plenty of room for my wool socks, though. What are you going to wear tomorrow?"

Christy noticed that all three girls had turned their backs on Katie and were gathered around Christy. It made her feel nervous and on the spot. Not at all like the center of attention in a popular way.

"Well, I, um . . . I guess some ski clothes. We're going skiing first thing in the morning, aren't we?"

"We leave at six-thirty," Katie said.

The three girls ignored her.

"Six-thirty," Christy repeated. "Boy, that's early. Guess we'd better get some sleep. I think I'll go get my sleeping bag ready." Christy gently broke out of the cocoon surrounding her and headed for the door.

"Girls?" Janet called, coming down the stairs. "I have everything set up for making tomorrow's lunches. Could you come and help me?"

"Sure," Christy said, eager to change locations. "What can we do?"

Katie joined her, taking the stairs two at a time. The others followed slowly behind.

Janet explained the assembly line she had set up on the kitchen counter. "Everyone gets one sandwich. Try to get two sandwiches out of each packet of lunch meat."

"I don't eat processed meat," Tiffany said, her arms folded in front of her.

"I remembered that from last year, Tiffany. I brought peanut butter and jelly especially for you."

Tiffany made a face.

Janet went on with her instructions. "We need to make a total of fourteen lunches. Here's a felt-tip pen to put names on them. At the end of the counter by the lunch bags is a box of apples. Here are the cookies, and drinks are in the ice chest. Any questions?"

"Let's make a production line," Katie said. "I'll start down here with the bread and mayonnaise. Christy, why don't you be the meat slapper?"

"The meat slapper," Shannon mimicked, and the three girls laughed.

Christy moved into position and bravely said, "Okay, one meat slapper coming up."

The other three reluctantly began to write names on the lunch sacks and stuff cookies into plastic bags.

Katie tried to pry the lid off the mayonnaise jar. It was stubborn and didn't cooperate with her muscular twists and turns. Shannon came over to see what was holding up the line.

"Here," she said. With a flick of her acrylic nail, the plastic seal broke loose.

At the same moment, the lid popped off due to the change in altitude. A spray of mayonnaise squirted out the side, splattering Katie's face and shirt.

It was a hilarious sight, and without thinking, Christy blurted out, "You have to be smarter than the mayonnaise jar, Katie."

All the girls burst into a chorus of laughter, while Katie fumbled for a paper towel to wipe off her face. *Why did I say that? Where did it come from? I didn't mean to humiliate her in front of these girls.*

The girls laughed much longer than the joke deserved. By the look on Katie's face, Christy knew she had done some major damage to Katie's feelings. Christy quietly worked on divvying up the lunch meat.

The lunches were completed with a lot of chatter and uninvited directions from the guys, who suddenly appeared and gave special orders on how they liked their sandwiches. Christy kept quiet, afraid her rough tongue might rebel on her once more before the night was over.

Maybe Janet assumed Christy's silence was a result

of the guys' taunting, because she sidled up behind Christy and whispered, "Tomorrow night they'll make the sandwiches, and you can get even by bossing them around."

Christy smiled and let Janet think that's what she was clammed up about. She finished her part of the lunch making and slipped out of the group so she could go down to her room and get ready for bed. Katie came in about ten minutes later and silently laid out her sleeping bag.

"Katie?" Christy said softly, already in her sweats, with her hair back in a clip and her face freshly washed. "Katie, I'm sorry I said that. I apologize."

"That's okay," Katie said without looking up from her bed preparations. "Don't worry about it. I deserved it."

"I still had no right to say it, and I'm sorry. Will you please forgive me?"

Katie looked up slowly. A smile forced its way across her face. "Sure. I forgive you. Don't worry about it."

Christy probably would have lain awake for a long time rehashing the whole situation, except she was so tired, the minute her head hit the pillow she was gone.

A shrill alarm clock startled her into an upright position. Her eyes darted around the dark room. It took her a while to remember where she was.

"It's five-thirty, you guys," Julie announced from the other bed. "Who wants in the shower first?"

"I'll be second," mumbled Katie. "Give me five more minutes of sleep."

"I'll go," Christy volunteered, realizing this might be her only chance with so many girls getting ready. She felt like her head was full of cotton balls. All the early-morning noises seemed to bounce off her. She was quick in the shower and tried to be quick with the blow dryer, since it seemed as though the noise would wake up the whole building. With a towel around her, she returned to the darkened room and tried not to trip over Katie while searching for her duffel bag.

"You done?" Katie muttered.

"It's all yours," Christy whispered back. "Do you mind if I turn on a light?"

"Go ahead," Julie said from the bed. "We need to get going." Then she added to Katie, "I hope you're as fast in the shower as your friend."

The light snapped on, and Christy felt awkward standing there with only a towel on, and the other three girls sitting up in bed looking at her. She quickly pulled out one of her new ski outfits. It was the black pants and pink and black jacket. By the time Katie returned from her shower, Christy was dressed and ready to go.

The other two girls took their turns in the bathroom. Katie suggested that she and Christy help with breakfast since they had extra time waiting for everyone else to be ready.

Upstairs they found Mr. Riley and his wife putting out bowls and spoons on the table. On the stove the tea kettle whistled.

"Good morning, early birds!" Mr. Riley said. "I'll go see if the guys are ready. You two can help yourselves to some instant oatmeal."

"There's also juice and donuts," Janet added. "And hot chocolate and hot apple cider if you want something to warm you before we face the icicles outside."

Within twenty minutes everyone had made an appearance at the breakfast table. Some ate, others only grabbed their lunches and stuck a donut between their teeth as the group loaded into the van.

No doubt about it, it was cold. It took eight attempts before the engine on the poor van could turn over. Everyone huddled on the cold, vinyl van seats, rubbing their hands and exhaling great puffs of air.

Christy did a final check in her day pack for her goggles, Chap Stick, and wallet. She found she had everything except her courage. Somehow, she had thought if she made it this far in the process, the adrenaline would kick in, and she would feel wild and daring. She only felt cold and nervous.

"You look so cute," Shannon commented from her seat behind Christy. "I love your outfit."

"Thanks," Christy said.

Then, as if Katie weren't sitting there, Shannon added, "And Katie must be wearing another one of your outfits. I love the sweater."

Christy glanced at Katie, then back at Shannon. All she could do was meekly say, "Thanks."

During the next half hour Christy played different scenarios over in her mind. She told herself that many people skied all the time, and not all of them broke bones. Some of them must even like skiing, because they apparently kept coming back every year. If she started to go too fast on the skis, she could always sit down in the snow. That seemed like a safe technique. After all, how dangerous could ski lessons be?

By the time she and Katie were outfitted with boots, skis, and poles, it was almost nine and time for ski school. They were the only two from the group who were taking lessons. Christy felt thankful for the time to be alone with Katie, without all the pressure from the other girls.

They took the gondola by themselves to the ski school location and followed the signs to where their class was to meet on the side of a slightly sloping hill.

The sun had broken through the morning clouds, and everything around them looked ultra-bright as the sunlight reflected off the snow. The girls carried their skis and crunched through the snow. They took their places with the nine other students, who were of all ages, shapes, and sizes.

"Yoo-hoo!" called a voice from the ski lift overhead. "Have fun, you two!"

They looked up and saw Mr. and Mrs. Riley on their way to the mountaintop, their ski-fitted feet swaying below their wooden seat.

Christy waved. Katie fumbled for her goggles to

block the bright sun and asked, "Was that Janet?"

Christy nodded and asked, "Do you think we'll ever graduate from ski school and be brave enough to actually ride in one of those things all the way to the top?"

"I'm counting on it," Katie said. "So, where's our ski instructor?"

"Right here," said a deep voice behind them.

They turned and saw a tall, tanned, smiling guy who looked the epitome of every girl's dream of a ski instructor.

"Maybe I don't want to be in such a big hurry to graduate," Katie whispered.

"I'm Dawson," the guy said, addressing the group of novices. "I'll be your instructor today. The first thing we'll work on is how to put on your skis."

What Christy would have guessed to be an easy procedure turned out to be awkward. It took everyone in the class four or more tries before each of them managed to get the skis on. With their poles holding them steady, the class waited for further instruction.

Dawson began with showing them how to stop, demonstrating how to point the skis in a pie or wedge shape, how to balance, and how to plant the poles in the snow for support. Next the class was shown how to walk sideways up a hill. They all began to practice.

"So far so good," Christy said to Katie.

"I don't know about you," Katie said, "but I think I might need some personal instruction after class. You know, some up-close-and-personal instruction."

"Okay, that's good!" Dawson called out. "Everyone stop where you are. Now try turning halfway around, keeping your skis together in a wedge. Remember, balance. Stay in control."

Christy lifted one long ski and put it down. But it landed across the top of the ski on her left foot. She lifted the right one again and pointed it straight. She tried to lift the left foot. As soon as she did, the right ski began to move forward. She quickly put her left foot down. Now both skis were beginning to move, and both were pointed straight downhill, right at Dawson.

"Yikes!" Christy called out. "Stop me, Katie!"

Katie lunged her hand forward in an effort to grab Christy's leg. Instead, the point of her ski pole made contact, slicing a two-inch hole in the right side of Christy's ski pants.

Christy kept moving downhill, picking up speed.

"Plant your poles! Wedge your feet!" Dawson yelled.

Christy tried everything at once, but in her panic she lost all sense of balance. Shrieking, lurching, and flailing her arms, Christy sped forward, running face-first into Dawson's chest.

It seemed his firm stance was enough to break her fall. The problem was, Christy's skis had slid between Dawson's legs, which were planted in a firm A-frame. Even though her face had stopped with as much finesse as if it had hit a brick wall, her legs kept going, pulling the rest of her body with them.

Just as she was about to slip between his legs and slide down the rest of the hill on her backside, Dawson grabbed her under both arms and pulled her back to an upright position.

"You okay?" he asked, his arms still supporting her, their faces only inches apart.

"I, I think so."

"Hey, Christy!" came a call from the overhead ski lift.

Christy looked up and saw Shannon waving her camera and yelling, "I captured that one on film."

Dawson smiled.

Christy smiled back, letting out a nervous giggle. "Sorry!"

"No problem. Now I'm going to let go of you and step to the side. I want you to try sidestepping back up to the rest of the class. Think you can try that?"

Christy laughed nervously again and said the only thing that came to mind. "Guess I have to be smarter than the skis, huh?"

"You're doing fine," Dawson said without laughing at her dumb joke. "Try to remember to balance this time. There you go. You've got it."

Christy sidestepped uphill while the rest of the class watched. As soon as she managed to make her way back into the line ncxt to Katie, Katie said, "Very sneaky!"

"I did not do that on purpose! You know that."

"You'll never convince me of that, you ski-instructor-stealer, you!"

"Hey, be my guest. He's all yours!" Christy teased back. "Try the same thing I did. If you like running into a brick wall at full speed, with an audience, my technique works great!"

"Maybe I'll wait until lunch and see if he wants to join me for cookies and cocoa," Katie said. "What do you think? Does he look like the cookie-type or the apple-type?"

Christy adjusted her goggles and rubbed her sore nose. "Bricks. He looks like the bricks-and-cement-type. Believe me, I'm speaking from the up-close-and-personal viewpoint. The guy eats bricks."

Chapter 11

A Little Mouthwash Goes a Long Way

By lunchtime Dawson had disappeared, and Christy and Katie were on their own with their sack lunches and cups of hot cocoa. After removing their skis and getting their booted feet back on solid ground, they found a picnic table and reviewed for each other the morning's events.

"Can I just say that you were about the funniest looking snow bunny I've ever seen?" Katie asked.

"Oh, well, you were a lot of help. Trying to harpoon me with your ski pole!" Christy ran her finger over the tear in her ski pants. "The purpose of ski poles is to balance yourself, not skewer your neighbor."

Katie laughed and said, "You should have seen the look on Dawson's face when you were coming at him! Did you see him?"

"No, I was too busy trying to 'wedge,' and then all I could do was examine the fine-gauge knit on his ski sweater."

"Up close and personal," Katie quipped.

"Very up close and personal," Christy said, still laughing. "I felt like a total klutz!"

"Well, can I just say that you—"

Christy cut in and finished the sentence for her, "—I looked like a total klutz."

"How did you know that's what I was going to say?" Katie asked.

"A wild hunch."

"I can see the report on TV tonight," Katie teased. "Innocent ski instructor maimed for life by a total klutz—news at eleven."

They both laughed until the cold air stung the tears in their eyes.

"You have to admit," Christy said, "that for our first time ever on skis, we didn't do too badly."

"We?"

"Okay, you didn't do too badly. And I conquered a whole bunch of fears. I'm willing to try again after lunch."

"Should be easy to find our ski instructor. He's the one with the indentation on his sweater in the shape of Christy's goggles." Katie said. They burst into another round of laughter.

"He's probably going to run when he sees us coming back for more," Christy said.

"When he sees *you* coming back for more. I, so far, have not yet had an up-close-and-personal encounter with the guy. However, the day isn't over yet!"

"We make a great tag team," Christy said. "I'll terrorize him in the morning class; you terrorize him in the afternoon class. Maybe they'll give us a brand new instructor tomorrow morning, and we can start the relay all over again!"

As soon as Katie stopped laughing, she pulled her sandwich out of her bag and said, "We should have at least insisted on turkey. It is Thanksgiving, you know."

"That's right! I wonder if my family has eaten yet. Probably not. We always go for a long walk while the turkey bakes. It's weird not being there. Happy Thanksgiving, Katie."

"Happy Thanksgiving to you too. And thanks for coming on this trip with me. It's exactly what I thought skiing would be like."

"Katie, we haven't exactly skied yet."

"All in good time, Christy. We have two more days of this."

"How many ski instructors is that, if I keep up my present rate of mutilation?" Christy asked.

Katie laughed so hard, she nearly choked on her sandwich.

In spite of all their joking, they both did well in their afternoon ski class. Christy, however, felt ready to turn in her skis by three and let her aching legs have a rest.

They met the group back at the van at four-thirty and humbly listened to everyone else tell exciting stories of swooshing down Siberian Express, Shirley Lake, and some of the other more treacherous runs. Somehow, Christy's announcing that she had completed her first successful snowplow didn't seem like worthy news.

Mr. Riley drove to a Mexican restaurant at the Boatworks in Tahoe City, and the group waited twenty minutes before being seated at a long table.

The baskets of chips were instantly devoured, and everyone ordered combination plates. The conversation flowed in and around Christy. From her seat between Katie and Mr. Riley, she found it easier to listen to all the clamor rather than to try to jump in and add to it. It seemed that everyone was having a great time.

When they arrived back at the condos, there wasn't a lot of complaining when Mr. Riley asked everyone to go right to bed so they could be ready to leave at six-thirty again the next morning.

Christy headed for her bed, eager to make contact with her pillow. But Shannon called to her from the other bedroom, where the three girls were sitting on the floor, pulling off their boots and rubbing their feet.

"We want you to come skiing with us tomorrow," Shannon said. "We've all talked about it, and we'll only take you on the bunny slopes until you're ready for more."

"I kind of already decided to go back to ski school with Katie tomorrow," Christy said. "I'm not very good yet."

"Yes, you are," Shannon protested. "We saw you, and you're good enough to try a bigger hill."

"You saw me all right! You saw me colliding with the poor ski instructor. By the way, I want that picture and the negative when you have it developed."

"I hope it comes out," Shannon said with a giggle. "It was kind of funny."

"Will you come with us tomorrow?" Jennifer asked.

"Maybe I could ski with you part of the day. I could attend ski school in the morning, and then Katie and I could come with you guys for the afternoon."

"We weren't exactly inviting Katie," Tiffany said. "We thought it would be more convenient with you because you'd make it a foursome, which makes it a whole lot easier on the lifts and everything."

"I guess I'll have to see how things go tomorrow," Christy answered cautiously. She didn't want to blow an opportunity to get "in" with these girls, but at the same time, she didn't want to put any strain on her relationship with Katie after they had had such a fun day together.

"Okay," Shannon agreed, "we'll meet you at the snack bar after your morning class, and you can tell us then."

For the last few minutes, Christy had been hiccuping. With each hiccup came the taste of Mexican food. "Can I get a drink in your bathroom?"

"Sure. Go ahead."

Christy twisted her head into the sink and drank out of the faucet, hoping to shake the hiccups. She noticed a bottle of mouthwash on the counter and called out,

"Is it okay if I use some of your mouthwash? I've heard that gargling sometimes helps hiccups."

"I don't think—" Jennifer began, but Shannon interrupted her.

"It's okay," Shannon said. "It's not really ours. It was here when we got here, but I'm sure you can use it."

Christy could hear the girls murmuring in the background as she took a quick swig of the green mouthwash and bent her head back to gargle.

Suddenly her throat was on fire. Her whole mouth felt torched. She quickly coughed and spit out the mouthwash. Then she stuck her mouth back under the faucet to let the cold water soothe the numbness.

Christy thought she heard one of the girls say, "I told you guys!"

She grabbed a towel to dry off her face but kept coughing. Her mouth still felt tingly. "What is that stuff?"

They all looked at each other. Tiffany sprang from the bed and said, "Why? What happened?"

The other girls followed her into the bathroom, where they joined Christy.

"I only tried to gargle with a little bit, but my whole mouth lit on fire!" Christy explained, still coughing. "I've never tasted a mouthwash like that before."

"I wonder what it could be?" Tiffany said. She opened the large bottle and sniffed its green contents.

"It doesn't really smell like anything. Maybe we should put it back under the counter where we found it," Tiffany suggested.

Her two friends agreed.

"I'm sure it's old or something. We probably should have left it there," Shannon said.

Tiffany was about to stash the bottle under the counter when Katie appeared. "There you are! I wondered where everyone went."

Spying the big bottle in Tiffany's hand, she said, "Are you having a bad-breath party, and you didn't invite me?"

"There's something wrong with it," Christy said. "I used some, and I felt as though I was about to choke to death."

"Really?" Katie said. "Let me smell it."

"We already smelled it," Shannon said briskly. "We're going to put it back where we found it. I don't think you should mess with it, Katie."

Undaunted, Katie reached over and took the bottle out of Tiffany's hand. "I'm only going to smell it, you guys. What's the big deal?"

She unscrewed the white lid and took a whiff. "Hmmm." She sniffed again.

Christy noticed that Shannon and the other girls were exchanging glances, which showed their obvious disapproval of Katie.

Katie stuck her finger into the bottle and tasted the green liquid. "Vodka," she announced. "It's not mouthwash at all! Someone filled this bottle with vodka and added green food coloring to make it look like mouthwash."

Christy was shocked.

Shannon looked at Christy and then said, "Who would do such a thing? It was here when we got here, right girls?"

The other two agreed, and Katie said, "I think we should give the bottle to Janet right now."

"Good idea," Tiffany said, grabbing the bottle back and tightly screwing on the lid. "I'll take it to her."

"Let's all take it up," Katie suggested. "We can go right now."

"We'll do it later," Tiffany said firmly. "The guys are up there now making lunches for tomorrow, and I don't want to cause a big scene."

Christy thought the reasoning sounded legitimate, but Katie wasn't buying it. "So what if the guys are there? I say we take it up now."

"Look," Shannon said firmly, "we said we'd turn it in, and we will."

Jennifer stepped between Shannon and Katie and said, "Katie, you don't understand. You and Christy didn't go on this trip last year. The three of us did. You see, last year they had some problems. I don't want it to appear that we're going to cause any trouble this year."

"What kind of problems?" Katie asked.

"Several couples came last year, and Mr. Riley found they were sneaking off at night to be together, if you know what I mean."

"What does that have to do with us finding a bottle

of green vodka?" Katie challenged.

"You don't understand. Last year Mr. Riley found out at four in the morning what was going on. He woke up everyone, had us pack all our stuff, and drove us back home after only one day of skiing. It ruined the weekend."

"I remember hearing about that," Katie said.

"So, don't you see?" Jennifer pleaded. "If he even thought this bottle of liquor was ours, he could cancel the rest of the trip right here and now. Everyone would be super mad at us for making a big deal over nothing."

"I think the best thing for us to do is pour it down the drain ourselves and not say anything about it," Shannon suggested.

"Great idea," Tiffany said, gently nudging the girls out of the bathroom with one hand while still holding the bottle in the other hand. "If you all will excuse me, I need to use the restroom."

Before Christy knew it, Tiffany had pushed them all out of the bathroom, and they stood together in the bedroom, looking at each other.

"I don't know about you guys," Jennifer said, "but I'm ready for a good night's sleep. Good night, Christy and Katie."

"Good night," they both said on their way down the hall to their room.

Katie switched on the light, and their two roommates, who were already in bed, cried out, "Hey, do you mind?"

With a snap the light was off, and Katie led Christy to their adjacent bathroom.

Once inside with the door closed, Katie turned on the light and whispered to Christy, "I know they're lying."

"How can you say that?"

"I know they are. They brought the vodka. I just know it."

"They said they found it under the counter when they got here," Christy protested. "If they brought it, and it was supposed to be a big secret, then why did they leave it out on the counter?"

"Because it's camouflaged in that bottle and with the green food coloring. They never expected you to use it. Didn't they act a little hesitant when you opened the bottle?"

"Not that I remember," Christy said. "They said they would pour it out, and I think we should believe them and trust them. If they don't pour it out, then we can tell Janet. I'd hate to be blamed for ruining this whole trip over a misunderstanding."

"You're too trusting, Christy. You're only worried about your precious reputation with those girls, aren't you?"

"What's that supposed to mean?" Christy said, raising her voice.

"I mean, you want them to like you so much you're willing to believe a lie!"

"I am not! I'm trying to give them the benefit of the doubt. You're too judgmental; that's your problem!"

"Judgmental! Ha!" Katie spouted.

Before Katie could finish, Christy put her hand on Katie's shoulder and said, "Wait a minute. I'm sorry. I take that back. I don't want to get in a fight with you. We've never fought like this before, Katie, and I don't want to start now."

Katie's red face slowly toned down its shade. "You're right," she said. "We shouldn't be arguing. Those girls are the problem, not you and me."

"Actually," Christy said, taking a deep breath and trying to calm down, "I think the problem is that we're supposed to be witnessing to those girls, and we've ended up being divided over them."

"You're right again," Katie said, all the fire extinguished from her eyes. "You're probably right, too, about the judgmental part. I tend to form hard-and-fast opinions of people."

"I shouldn't have said anything. I'm sorry. And you're probably right about my being too trusting. I tend to be too naive about things. I mean, I practically drank the stuff and choked on it, but I never would have known it was vodka. I've never tasted anything like that before."

"You know," Katie said, "I think there's a way for us both to find out if they're telling the truth or not."

"How?"

Katie's green eyes narrowed to catlike slits. "Listen," she said, "I have a plan."

Chapter 12

Traitor

The next morning, Christy and her roommates followed the same wake-up routine as the day before. After Katie and Christy dressed, they went upstairs and helped Janet prepare breakfast.

The guys made their appearance first, followed at last by the rest of the girls. The kitchen was a muddled flurry of breakfast preparations and lunch-bag sorting.

Christy made eye contact with Katie across the room and nodded her head once. Katie then slipped away from the group and disappeared downstairs.

"Did you get your lunch yet, Christy?" Janet asked, startling her out of her concentration.

"Oh, no. Thanks. I'll get it."

"There's one more bag," Janet said, turning it so she could see the name. "Katie," she read aloud. Looking around, she asked, "Where is Katie?"

"I'll take it for her," Christy offered.

Shannon apparently overhead Janet asking Christy about Katie. She called to Christy from the kitchen table, "Where is Katie? Did she give up on skiing after yesterday's lessons? Is she going to stay in bed all day?"

"No," Christy answered, her heart pounding. "She's going. She just had to go downstairs for a minute."

Shannon turned, whispered something to Tiffany, and then hopped up from her chair and hurried down the stairs.

Oh, no! Katie, look out! Shannon's going to catch you snooping.

Christy quickly slipped around the counter to the kitchen and flipped on the garbage disposal switch. Immediately everyone stopped their conversations and turned to look at her.

"Oops!" Christy said, shrugging her shoulders. "Wrong switch."

Just then Katie appeared at the top of the stairs and looked around the room anxiously until she spotted Janet. Motioning for Christy to follow her, Katie went over to where Janet sat at the table and leaned down to say something to her in private.

Janet rose from her chair and led Katie to her room. Christy waited until they came her direction before she joined the procession. All the while she was aware of Tiffany and Jennifer, who were still seated at the table, watching Katie's every move.

Just as Christy slipped into Janet's room, she noticed Tiffany and Jennifer heading down the stairs. Janet closed the door, and Katie started in breathlessly. She sounded like a spy who had returned from a successful secret mission.

"I found it," Katie said to Christy. "And I was right.

They didn't empty it out. It wasn't under the sink, and that's why it took me so long to find it. I got your signal, though. Thanks!"

"Would you mind backing up here?" Janet asked. "I seem to have missed something."

Katie talked fast, using her hands and expressive facial gestures. She explained how the "rich girls" had a bottle of vodka in their room, and how even though they said they were going to pour it out, the bottle was still there this morning.

"So you found the full bottle just sitting on their bathroom counter?" Janet asked.

"No, it was in the shower. I almost didn't see it, but then when Christy turned on the garbage disposal I knew that was the signal someone was coming. I turned around really fast and spotted it through the shower's glass door. I barely made it out of there before Shannon came in."

"Why didn't you girls tell me all this last night?"

"They said they would pour it out, and I believed them," Christy said.

Katie gave her an I-told-you-so look.

"We can't let this go," Janet said. "Not after what happened last year. You girls stay here. I'll get Lou, and we'll bring the other girls in too."

Christy sat on the edge of the bed with Katie beside her. Her hands were shaking, and she felt her throat closing up. She hated being in situations like this. Why hadn't those girls kept their word and poured out the stuff? Was it actually their bottle of camouflaged vodka after all? Was Katie right about them?

Mr. Riley entered the room with Janet and the three girls and closed the door behind him. All five of the girls crowded onto the bed. Christy focused on her hands folded in her lap, not willing to look anyone in the eye.

"Katie says you girls had a bottle of vodka in your room last night. What do you have to say about that?" Mr. Riley asked, his arms folded across his chest.

Shannon, looking innocent and offended by the accusation, said, "It was a bottle of mouthwash we found under our sink. Christy had some, and it made her cough, and then Katie came bursting into our bathroom and said it was vodka with green food coloring."

"Was it?" Janet asked.

"How would we know? We didn't try it," Shannon said.

"Where's the bottle now?" Mr. Riley asked.

"We poured it out and threw the bottle away last night. We didn't want any misunderstandings, like last year," Jennifer answered.

"That's not true!" Katie burst out. "The full bottle is still in your bathroom. I saw it in the shower this morning!"

"What were you doing in our bathroom?" Tiffany asked.

"Checking to see if you kept your word, which you didn't," Katie stated firmly.

Christy felt more and more uncomfortable as the accusations continued. She didn't know what to say.

"Let's all go downstairs and have a look in your bathroom. We'll settle this once and for all," Mr. Riley said, opening the door.

Don was standing right next to the door, apparently listening to the conversation.

"Oh, hey!" Don said when Mr. Riley opened the door. "We were just going to ask how soon until we load up the van. It's almost seven o'clock."

"We'll leave in about ten minutes," Mr. Riley said. "Excuse us." Pressing past the eager skier, Mr. Riley led the parade of girls downstairs.

The seven of them squeezed into the bathroom.

"Okay, Katie," Mr. Riley said, "where did you see the bottle of mouthwash?"

"In the shower," she said. "Behind the glass door there."

Mr. Riley opened the shower door and picked up a bottle filled with green liquid. He held it up for his wife to see and read the label, "Herbal Garden Shampoo. You used to use this brand, didn't you, Janet?"

She nodded and said, "Maybe you should take the lid off and smell it."

"It wasn't shampoo," Katie protested. "It was mouthwash. A big bottle, and it was in there this morning."

Christy watched as the three girls looked at each other, shrugging their shoulders and exchanging expressions of innocence.

Mr. Riley twisted off the lid from the shampoo and poked his finger inside. Rubbing his thumb and fingers together until they formed a lather, he sniffed at the liquid and said, "This is shampoo, Katie. One hundred percent shampoo."

"I know," Katie said, exasperated. "I'm talking about mouthwash, not shampoo. Check under the cupboards and in their luggage. It was here twenty minutes ago."

"Christy," Mr. Riley said, turning to her, "what was it that you drank last night?"

Feeling all eyes on her, Christy said, "I didn't really drink anything. I was trying to gargle. See, I had the hiccups, and I came in here to get a drink of water. I saw the mouthwash on the counter and asked the girls if I could have some."

"And they didn't try to stop you or say, 'That's not mouthwash'?" Mr. Riley asked.

"No, I mean, I don't think so. I don't remember. I just took a little bit, and my mouth felt on fire so I spit it out and rinsed my mouth with water."

"It got rid of her hiccups," Shannon said with a smile.

"You don't know if it was vodka or not, though, do you?" Janet asked.

"No, I've never tasted vodka before, or anything like that, so I don't know what it tastes like," Christy said.

"Katie was the one who drank some and said it was vodka," Shannon offered.

"I didn't drink any. I only tasted it since it didn't have much of a smell."

"Okay, okay," Mr. Riley said, looking irritated and putting the shampoo back in the shower. "Where is the mouthwash bottle now?"

"There," Shannon said pointing to the trash can. "Since Katie made such a big deal over it last night, we poured it out and threw the bottle away."

Mr. Riley lifted the empty bottle from the trash can, untwisted the lid and sniffed. "Nothing," he said, handing the white cap to Janet. "It doesn't smell like anything. I don't know what was in here."

Janet smelled the cap and shook her head. "It seems like a big hassle over nothing. It's poured out, and that's all that matters. I'm no psychologist, but I'd say maybe, just maybe, you girls are quarreling over something else here. Something completely unrelated, like territory or friendship loyalty. Can we drop this whole thing and finish the trip without any more hassles?"

"I agree," Mr. Riley said. "We've held up the whole group over this. I appreciate your concerns, Katie. Sounds like it was a case of someone leaving an old bottle of mouthwash under the sink for too long. You girls came along and happened to use some, and it had a kick to it. You poured it out and threw away the bottle and that's that."

"But, Mr. Riley," Katie said, looking frantic, "I know what I saw. You can't just drop the whole thing like this. Christy will back me up. I'm telling the truth."

Mr. Riley paused for a moment and looked at Christy. She froze under his intent gaze. "Do you honestly think it was vodka?" he asked.

Everyone was staring at her. All Christy could say was, "I don't know."

Turning to Katie, he said, "Maybe it's time to stop forcing the issue here. No rules have been violated. If you want to keep pressing it, then maybe I'll have to ask you why it is that you, a girl under the legal drinking age, even knows what vodka tastes like."

Then pointing his finger at the three girls in front of him, he said, "And if I find out that you do have liquor on this trip, you need to know, young ladies, that the consequences for all three of you will be extremely serious. Is that understood?"

"Yes, sir," they all answered, nearly in unison and with somber faces.

"Okay. Let's load up and get out of here. The snow is melting while we stand here bickering in the bathroom. This is crazy!"

They all filed out. Christy went to her room to retrieve her day pack and jacket. Katie was right behind her.

"Traitor," Katie muttered under her breath as she entered the room and slammed the door.

Christy felt as though her heart had just broken. Why would Katie say that to her? She started to cry and turned to face her angry friend.

"Why didn't you stick up for me?" Katie asked, tears now coming to her eyes too. "You made me look like a donkey in front of everyone, and you know I was right!

Why didn't you tell them it was vodka?"

"Katie, all I could say was the truth. I don't know what it was! I don't know what vodka tastes like. I was not trying to betray you! How can you say that to me? I only told the truth!"

Katie wiped her eyes with the back of her hand. With quick, jerking motions she yanked off the black and white ski sweater and peeled off the black ski pants.

"I don't feel like wearing these today," she said, throwing the ski clothes onto Christy's bed. Grabbing a pair of jeans and a red sweat shirt, she stormed into the bathroom and slammed the door.

Christy wanted to throw herself on the bed and cry her eyes out. But from the hallway she heard Don yelling for everyone to hurry up because it was already seven-thirty. Numbly gathering her things, she wiped her eyes and headed for the door.

Chapter 13

Guilty

Christy spent the rest of the morning in ski class with Katie. Yet they couldn't bring themselves to speak to each other.

How can it be that I'm only a few feet from my closest friend, but I've never been so lonely in my life? This has to be the most horrible, miserable, alienating experience ever! What am I going to do? How can I mend things with Katie?

Cold, wet, and unable to concentrate, Christy excused herself from class and plowed her way back through the snow to the lodge. She went to her locker and pulled out her day pack, in search of a tissue for her leaky nose. No such luck. The bathroom was close, and she was glad to find a tissue box in the wall near the paper towels.

Having blown her nose and taken a few extra tissues to stuff in her pocket, Christy was about to leave when she heard her name mentioned.

Someone behind one of the closed stalls said, "It was a good thing Christy was on our side, or else Mr. Riley might have believed Katie."

"Oh, I know!" a voice from another closed stall answered. "That little snoop almost ruined everything. Are you sure Christy's totally on our side?"

"I'm going to make sure before the day is over. She's supposed to go skiing with us this afternoon. I'm going to be super nice to her just to cement her friendship."

A stall door opened, and Christy froze, expecting it to be one of the girls. It wasn't. With her heart pounding, she slipped into the vacated stall to listen to the rest of the conversation.

She heard another stall door open, and from the way the voices moved and from the sound of running water, Christy guessed that at least one of the girls was out of the stall and over by the sink, washing her hands.

"Do you really think Christy has never tasted any liquor before? I mean, did you see her? She played innocent better than we did!"

"Who knows? She could be telling the truth. I don't know. At least she isn't a truth crusader like Katie."

"I don't think we have to worry about Katie anymore." The voice paused and then said, "Ugh! Why didn't you guys tell me my hair was such a mess! Did you bring a brush?"

"There's one in my locker. Come on. Let's pick up our lunches, and I'll get the brush for you."

"So, you really think we're not going to have any more problems with Katie?"

"To quote Christy on her classic line with the mayonnaise blow-out, 'You have to be smarter than the bottle of mouthwash, Katie!' "

"Then it looks like we're safe."

Muffled giggles followed the girls as they exited the bathroom.

Katie was right; it was vodka! And they sound as though they still have it! What should I do?

It seemed the only thing for Christy to do was meet the girls at lunch, as planned. Surely she would be able to think of some way to confront them with this whole thing then.

Throwing her day pack over her shoulder, Christy marched to the appointed meeting place at the snack bar. The girls weren't there yet so Christy decided to act casual, find a place to sit down, and start to eat her lunch. She settled in and unzipped her pack, only to find she had no lunch. She had left it back at the condo.

I don't believe this! This day keeps getting worse and worse. What next?

What came next was the appearance of Shannon, Tiffany, and Jennifer. She wasn't ready to face them.

"Hi!" Shannon called out, waving as she approached. "Did you forget your lunch? I saw it on the counter and brought it for you. Are you getting hungry?"

Christy smiled and meekly accepted her forgotten lunch. "Did you get Katie's too?"

"No, arc you sure she forgot hers? I only saw yours on the counter. Did I tell you how much I like your jacket? That color looks great on you."

Christy knew her lunch was right next to Katie's.

She was not in the mood to play any more games with these girls.

"Which run do you want to try first, Christy?" Tiffany asked. "Do you want to take it easy or dive right in and go to the top?"

"I'm still not sure," Christy replied, stalling. "I'm still signed up for ski school for the afternoon session."

"You're not going, are you? Why waste your time when you could be really skiing?" Shannon asked.

"Yeah," Jennifer added, "with us."

Christy bit into her sandwich so she wouldn't have to answer and slightly shrugged her shoulders.

I can't pretend I don't know what they said. I could find Janet and Mr. Riley, but then these girls would never speak to me again, and I'd feel awful.

Christy kept chewing slowly. *What am I thinking? Do I care what they think of me? No, I care about what Katie thinks of me. And I guess, ultimately, I care about what the Lord thinks of me. I have to say something. Lord, help!*

"Shannon," she blurted out, not sure of what she was going to say next, "um, can I ask your opinion on something?"

"Sure."

"Actually, I'd like it if all of you could give me your advice. I kind of have a problem."

"Does it start with 'K' and end with 'atie'?" Tiffany asked.

"I'll just say it's about a girl I know," Christy began,

still not sure of what she was doing, gingerly making it up as she went. One thing was certain—these girls loved to give advice. They had all stopped eating and were intently waiting to hear Christy's problem.

"This girl was sort of talked into buying some cosmetics from this friend of hers, who was trying to sell them," Christy began.

"We've all done that before, right?" Jennifer asked, and the others nodded in agreement.

"Well, this girl was told how great the products were, and if she didn't like them, she could return them anytime and get all her money back. So she tried them, and they didn't seem that great. But the friend who sold them to the girl kept flattering her and trying to make her feel good about it. About the cosmetics, I mean."

"That's how it usually goes," Jennifer commented. "Then what happened? Did she totally break out or what?"

"Actually," Christy continued, "the girl found out the cosmetic company was under investigation for fraud. Her friend promised that none of it was true, and she even tried to sell her some more of the stuff. The girl believed her friend and bought a bunch and even tried to convince some of her other friends that the products were good."

"What happened?" Jennifer asked.

"The girl accidentally overheard a conversation and found out that her friend had lied to her. The friend knew all along that the company was in trouble and the cosmetics weren't that good. She'd been using this girl the whole time."

"That is the lowest," Tiffany said. "I'd make the liar give me all my money back, and I'd never speak to her again."

"I'd sue the company," Shannon said.

"That's why I wanted your advice," Christy said. "Because the girl is thinking of going directly to the authorities and reporting the whole thing. Except she doesn't want to lose her friend who lied to her and used her. How can the girl work things out so that her friend won't use her anymore and yet expose the truth at the same time?"

The girls all looked at each other, and Shannon said, "Trash the friend! Go right to the authorities, and get justice."

"I agree," Jennifer said. "What kind of friend would set her up like that and keep up the front even when she knows it's a lie?"

"Friends like you," Christy blurted out.

"What are you talking about?" Shannon asked.

"Yeah, what is this? You're not talking about make-up, are you?" said Jennifer.

Christy forced herself to look directly at the girls and said, "I accidentally overheard you guys talking a little while ago in the bathroom. I know there really was vodka or some kind of liquor in the mouthwash bottle, that it was yours, and you still have it." Her voice began to quiver.

"And I don't know what to do about it. If I followed the advice you all just gave me, then I should go right to Mr. Riley and totally dump all of you as friends because you set me up, lied to me, and used me."

"We never lied, and we did not set you up," Shannon said. "You went for the mouthwash on your own. We didn't give it to you. Then we let the situation run its natural course. None of us told a lie."

"You're saying you honestly did find that bottle underneath the sink?" Christy questioned.

"Well, no," Tiffany admitted. "We had to make up that part. Except for that, we didn't lie."

Jennifer added, "If Katie hadn't come snooping around, everything would have smoothed over, and no one would have gotten hurt."

"Well, I got hurt," Christy said, feeling her emotions rising. She wasn't sure she could push them down much longer. "And I'll be honest with you guys—I don't know what I'm going to do about it. Your advice to me was to go right to the authorities and throw away the friendship. That might be the best advice, but I don't want to throw away any of my friendships—not with Katie and not with you."

Because she thought she was going to burst into tears or throw up or both, Christy excused herself and fled for the refuge of the restroom. She emerged from the stall fifteen minutes later, having had a good, long, quiet cry in private.

The last thing she felt like doing was going back out on the ski slopes. Collecting all her gear and checking her red, puffy eyes in the mirror, she left the restroom and headed for the huge fireplace in the lodge.

Finding an empty chair, Christy planted herself near the tall window, with her feet pointing toward the fire. Outside, the afternoon sun was now hidden by a block of clouds that looked like they had aprons full of snow and were waiting for the signal before dumping it on the earth below.

Then, as if God gave the signal for the matronly clouds to gleefully shake empty their aprons, tiny snow babies began to float to their new homes. Some were eagerly adopted by the sturdy evergreens, stretching out their arms to receive them. Others caught rides on the shoulders of determined skiers snowplowing their way down to the lodge. Most of the silent snowflakes found their places on the slopes where they huddled together with those that had come before them.

Somehow it all has a purpose and a place, Christy thought, as she settled into her chair and watched the world outside turn white. *The only comforting part of this whole mess is that God knows the beginning and the end. I know He cares about what I'm feeling, and I know that somehow, every time, He works it out for His good. Everything has a purpose.*

"Did you give up?" a voice said behind her.

Christy turned around and saw Mr. Riley holding a cup of hot cocoa.

"Just taking a break," Christy said. "Looks a little too cold out there for me."

"It's getting colder, and the visibility up on top is pretty soupy," he said. "If the rest of the group ends up huddled by the fire here, we might as well go back to the condo. We could rent a couple of movies and make some popcorn."

"That sounds like fun," Christy said, smiling up at him.

"I'm glad you're here by yourself for a minute," Mr. Riley said. "I've thought about something, and I wanted to run it past you."

"Good, because I have something I wanted to talk to you about too," Christy said.

"I realized that when I smelled the lid of the mouthwash bottle this morning, it didn't have any kind of odor. If it had been filled with mouthwash, it would have smelled minty. I use that brand, and it's very minty. Christy, do you think there's any chance the bottle did have some kind of liquor in it?"

Christy readjusted her position in the chair and decided this was the moment to tell all.

Just then Katie's voice called out behind them, "Mr. Riley, your wife is looking for you." Katie apparently hadn't seen Christy in the chair at first, because when she did notice her, she added, "Oh, I didn't know you were busy."

"Tell Janet I'll be right there. Christy was about to tell me something."

"Then I guess I better leave you two alone," Katie said.

Christy could hear the bite in her tone. Katie was still hurting, and Christy knew she had every right to be.

"No, I'd like you to stay, Katie. I'd like you to hear this too."

Katie hung back, not looking at Christy. Waiting for Christy to speak, she took a stance that said, "I dare you to melt me."

Christy looked up at Mr. Riley and began. "Katie was right. There was vodka in the mouthwash bottle. It was probably there in the shower this morning, too, just like Katie said."

"Oh, fine!" Katie said, throwing her hands in the air. "Now you're on my side. What brought about the big change? Did your new friends suddenly dump you?"

Christy kept her gaze on Mr. Riley as she explained that she had told the truth during the confrontation. She honestly didn't know what she had tasted the night before. What changed her mind was when she over-heard the girls talking.

"I wasn't trying to discredit you at all this morning, Katie. I was only trying to say what was true." Christy kept looking at Katie until Katie finally made eye contact. As soon as Katie's bloodshot eyes met hers, Christy said, "I'm sorry."

"No, it's my fault," Katie said in a small voice. "I never should have doubted you were telling the truth.

Can you forgive me for calling you a traitor?"

"Of course. And can you forgive me for not being braver and standing by you when it really counted?"

Katie smiled and nodded. "Of course," she said, bending over and giving Christy a hug. "It takes a lot more than that to break up a couple of peculiar treasures like us."

"Well, if you two have managed to mend your friendship, I think I'll go find Janet, and we'll get this whole thing cleared up. Thanks, both of you, for your honesty. You'd be surprised how hard it is to find a high school student these days who tells the truth. My opinion of you both just shot up about 100 percent. I wish more of my students were like you two."

Chapter 14

I Just Wanted to Be Sure of You

Christy," Mom called softly, "wake up, Christy. You have some visitors."

Christy rolled over on the couch and squinted at Mom. "Did I fall asleep? What time is it?"

"It's four o'clock," Mom said. "You fell asleep right after we got back from church this morning. You know, it's probably a good thing you came home a day early from that ski trip, otherwise you wouldn't have made it through school tomorrow."

Christy sat up on the couch and untwisted her red ski sweater. "I really conked out, didn't I? Did you say someone was here?"

"Yes," Mom hesitated. "I think you might be surprised."

"Who is it?" Christy said, releasing her hair from its ponytail clip and quickly running her fingers through it. "Did Katie come by with Glen? She was hoping he'd stop by her house this afternoon."

"Why don't you come see," Mom said. "They're

out in front, talking to Dad."

Christy rose from the couch, slipped on her shoes, and ran a finger under each eyelid in case her Sunday morning makeup had smeared while she slept. Opening the front door, she stepped out onto the porch. She could hear her dad talking to someone around the corner of the house, but she couldn't see who it was.

Giving her hair one more quick shake and taking another tug at her sweater, she walked down the steps and curiously rounded the corner of the house.

"Rick? Doug? Hi! What are you guys doing here?"

"Whoa," Doug teased. "It's 'Sleeping Beauty, Part Two'! And don't you look like the sun-kissed snow bunny. Did you have a good time?"

Doug, her friend from two summers ago at the beach, had no qualms about stepping right up and giving her a big hug in front of her dad and Rick. Christy had never figured out whether Doug really was clueless or so genuine he had nothing to hide, and that's why he freely acted on his impulses.

Christy accepted his enthusiastic hug and then, because it only seemed right, she turned toward Rick. He hesitated at first, but gave her a noncommittal side-squeeze without saying anything.

The instant Rick put his arm around her, she smelled his cologne. She didn't know what kind it was, but it was the same heady fragrance he had worn on every date they had gone on.

Instantly she felt her stomach tighten and her heart

swell with mixed feelings. She could tell by Rick's nonverbal greeting that he was either embarrassed to touch her in front of her dad or else being here was all Doug's idea.

"Yeah." Christy tried to remember Doug's question. "The ski trip went well. Not great, but well."

"If you kids will excuse me," Dad said, holding up a screwdriver, "I'm trying to fix the recliner."

Poor Dad! I wonder if the chair will cooperate with him this time.

"Your dad said you came back a day early because a storm was coming, and you didn't want to get snowed in," Doug said, leaning casually against the side of his yellow truck, which he had parked in the driveway.

"That was part of it," Christy said, giving a quick run-down of the confrontation with the girls over the liquor and how they finally had confessed to bringing it with the expectation of having a party on the last night. "I guess the ski club had a similar problem last year with some couples who snuck off."

Rick snickered and said the first words to her since he had arrived. "Did those three girls happen to mention they were the ones who snuck out last year?"

"No," Christy said, "they didn't happen to mention that."

She cautiously shot a glance at Rick. It felt odd being here with him, with no warning that she would face him today. He looked the same: tall, broad-shouldered, with wavy dark hair and chocolate brown eyes.

Yet he looked a little different. Was it that he was somehow more reserved, or was he mad?

She would have liked to say so many things to him, but none of them seemed possible with Doug standing a few feet away. It especially felt awkward since Doug was Todd's best friend, and now Doug and Rick were sharing an apartment and going to school together at San Diego State.

What surprised her the most was that at this moment, Rick no longer seemed to have that strong, overpowering effect he had had on her in the past. But she felt a strong desire to be friends with Rick. Good friends.

"We were stopping by to pick up some of Rick's junk on our way back to school. I told him I couldn't be this close to you without saying hi," Doug said. "You sure look great! I'm glad to hear you're doing well. I like your hair that way too."

Christy sheepishly smoothed down her wild mane. She could feel Rick's stare as she faced Doug. Rick always told her she looked good in red. Funny how she just happened to be wearing a red sweater the afternoon he decided to pop back into her life. She thought of the gold "forever" bracelet on her right wrist and wondered if it showed under the cuff of the sweater.

Would Rick notice? Would it even matter to him? And was it possible he was the one who bought it back for her?

"Do you guys want to come in? Do you want something to drink or anything?" Christy asked.

"We probably should get going," Rick said. "We have to get back by six for God-Lovers."

"God-Lovers?" Christy repeated, trying to remember where she had heard that expression before.

"Yeah, God-Lovers," said Doug with a smile. "You like the name? I picked it out. It's a bunch of Christians who meet at our apartment every week. I've been doing the teaching, but tonight Rick is teaching for the first time." Doug gave him a playful punch in the arm. "Getting a little nervous there, buddy?"

Rick tagged him back, and the male sporting ritual began. Christy watched as the two competitive, over-six-foot-tall "little boys" sparred with each other in her driveway.

She couldn't believe how well Rick and Doug got along. She had only seen Todd in that "best bud" position with Doug. Todd and Rick were so different from each other, yet Doug seemed to get along great with both of them.

Guys sure do this friendship thing differently than girls do.

Competitive Rick appeared to emerge victorious from their round, which was not a surprise to Christy. She decided some things about him might never change.

"I'm sure glad you guys came by. Sorry you couldn't stay longer," she said, not feeling ready to say good-bye to either of them.

She would have loved to jump in the truck with

them and go down to San Diego to their God-Lovers fellowship. She would have loved to hear Rick lead a Bible study and see firsthand what was going on in his life. Could it be that he really was getting serious about God?

"We'll all have to get together and do something during Christmas break," Doug said. "Are you going to be around, Christy?"

"Yes, I'll be around. We should do that. It would be fun!"

Doug gave her another bear hug before hopping up into his truck's front seat. "You can come down and see us anytime. Or if you can't come, send cookies!"

Christy laughed.

"I'm serious," Doug said. "Remember those cookies you made for Todd and me last Christmas? Those were the best cookies I've ever had."

"I'll see what I can do," Christy said with a smile. "Oh, but wait! I don't have your address."

Doug scrounged underneath his seat for a piece of paper and pulled out an empty french-fry wrapper. "Here," he said, handing the wrapper to Rick along with a pen from his glove box. "Give her our address."

Rick scribbled down the address. When he handed it to Christy, she reached for the paper with her right hand, and her bracelet came into plain view.

She watched Rick's face for any indication that he had noticed. He seemed to be looking at it, but the only change on his face were the corners of his mouth, which moved slightly upward. He didn't look at her. He didn't say anything.

Without even a good-bye hug, Rick hopped up into the passenger side of the truck. He reached for his sunglasses on the dashboard, slipped them on, and rested his arm on the rim of the open window.

"Bye," Christy said, sad that they were leaving after such a short visit. "I'm glad you guys came by. Next time stay longer, okay?"

Doug revved up the engine. Right before he backed out of the driveway, he called out, "Don't forget about sending those cookies!"

"I won't," Christy said, waving the french-fry wrapper in the air. "I'll send you some. I promise!"

Rick held up his hand, all five fingers outstretched in a frozen wave, as they backed up and headed down the street. She couldn't read his expression because the dark glasses covered his eyes. Very unsettling.

The encounter left her full of questions. Rick didn't seem like his old, domineering self. He didn't really seem mad. Was he hurt? Was it hard for him to be around her with Doug there, since they hadn't talked in so long? Did he feel the same way that Christy did, that things weren't completely cleared up between them?

She decided to go inside and call Katie to get her opinion.

"She's not here," Katie's brother said when Christy called.

"Could you please tell her I called, and I'll see her tomorrow at school?"

The next morning, as Christy grabbed her lunch off the counter on her way to school, Mom said, "Why don't you take that post office notice with you and pick up your package? I didn't get there this weekend."

Christy had forgotten all about the mystery package from 96817. She found the slip, stuck it in her purse, and rushed out the door.

In English class, her teacher finally handed back their essays on "A True Friend Is. . .". Christy got a B-, with a note that said, "Try working a little harder on sentence structure."

This shouldn't have been that hard. Why is it so tough for me to put my feelings into words? I guess it doesn't help much that I'm being graded for sentence structure instead of what I said.

The teacher gave them the last fifteen minutes of class to work on their next reading assignment. Christy pulled out her book and began to read, determined to finish in class so she wouldn't have more homework.

The girl behind Christy tapped her on the shoulder and slipped her a note. It was from Katie, and it said, "Do you want to read my paper? I got an A!!!"

Christy turned her head in Katie's direction and, with a smile, nodded her head. The paper was passed up to Christy while the teacher wrote on the board.

Sure enough, at the top of the page was a big A. Katie's first line was a quote:

"Piglet sidled up to Pooh.

"'Pooh!' he whispered.

"'Yes, Piglet?'

"'Nothing,' said Piglet, taking Pooh's paw. 'I just wanted to be sure of you.' "

Her paper went on to describe a true friend as someone who is there for you all the time, no matter what. Someone you don't have to impress because you always know you can be yourself, and that person will still accept you. She even quoted Proverbs 17:17, "A friend loves at all times."

The last few lines of Katie's paper said, "I feel I am more blessed than many people because I have this kind of a friend in my life. A friend who is always there for me no matter what. A friend who accepts me as I am but loves me too much to let me stay that way. Yes, I would say I am blessed because I have a true friend."

Christy bit her lower lip, feeling self-conscious and guilty. She didn't exactly measure up to all the qualities that Katie had listed as true-friend characteristics. She *would* be a better friend to Katie.

Christy handed the paper back to Katie at lunch and said, "It's really good. I have to tell you that it made me feel guilty though."

"Why?" Katie asked.

"The way you described your true friend as always being there for you and accepting you in every situation . . . ," Christy hesitated. "I mean, that's really a strong statement."

"You think it was too strong? I thought I watered it down too much," Katie said, examining the paper. "I even changed the last line before I handed it in. At first I had, 'I have a true friend, and His name is Jesus Christ.' But then I thought she might lower my grade."

Oh! That makes sense. The Lord is always there, and all those other things Katie wrote about Him are true too. Man, am I arrogant or what, to think Katie wrote about me!

"By the way," Katie said, "can you give me a ride home today? My brother borrowed my car again."

"I'll have to call my mom and ask, but I'm sure it'll be okay. I have to stop by the post office anyway. I received this strange notice that a package was sent to me with postage due."

"It's probably that free sample of sunscreen we sent away for last summer," Katie suggested. "I still haven't gotten mine."

"Could be," Christy said.

"What? You think it's from Rick or something?"

"No. Oh! I didn't tell you yet! Did your brother mention I called last night?"

"Mr. Message Messer-upper? No, not likely."

"Where were you? Did Glen come by?"

"No, I was at the grocery store with my mom. Glen didn't even call. Or maybe he did, and my brother forgot to give me the message. I'll see Glen Wednesday night at Bible study, and I'll find out then. Why did you call?"

"No big reason. Only to tell you that Rick and Doug came by yesterday."

Katie stopped eating her sandwich, and her eyes grew huge. "Why didn't you tell me? What happened? Did he notice your bracelet?"

Christy gave a detailed rundown of the situation.

Katie presented her evaluation. "If you ask me, Rick is still hurting over your breaking up with him. And, if you want my opinion on that, it was good for the boy. About time someone showed him what it feels like."

"That's not why I broke up with him."

"You broke up with him because he was a jerk, right?"

"No, Katie. He's not a jerk. He's just Rick."

"Same thing," Katie muttered.

"No, it isn't. It's hard to explain why I broke up with him. At the time it was based a lot on my feelings, and I knew I was doing the right thing. The only way I can describe it is Rick didn't have a spiritual dimension to him, and I really missed that, since Todd is 90 percent spiritual and 10 percent emotions. Rick was like 90 percent emotions, and I don't know how much of anything else. But when I saw him yesterday, he seemed more spiritual. He definitely wasn't the same guy. I think Doug has been a good influence on him."

"That's great! Really, I mean it. I know we're not supposed to judge, but with Rick it always seemed as though he was playing Christian. You couldn't tell if it was real to him, or if it was all stuff he was role-playing, since he'd been going to that church ever since he was a baby."

"I'd like to believe it's becoming real to him," Christy said. "That's what I'm going to start praying for. I put Jennifer, Shannon, and Tiffany on my prayer list. Maybe I should add Rick too."

"The one you should be praying for is Todd," Katie said. "You never heard back from him after you sent that card, did you?"

"No."

"Don't look like that, Christy."

"Like what?"

"You have that look that says, 'Todd has forgotten about me, and I'm never going to see him again in my entire life.' You know that's not true," Katie chided.

"Sometimes it's hard to know what's true," Christy said, trying not to sound sad. She looked down and spun her bracelet around her wrist. "I guess it's all the stuff on the true friends essays and being reminded of it today. I guess I feel like Piglet. Sometimes I just want to be sure of Pooh, you know what I mean?"

"Yeah, I know what you mean. But the Lord is the only one who is always going to be there for us every single time. You know that."

"I know that about the Lord, but I never know what to think about Todd."

"If you want my opinion . . . ," Katie hesitated.

Christy smiled and said, "You know I always want your opinion, or at least almost always."

Katie smiled back and said, "Well, whether you want it or not, my opinion on Todd is that you should always go back to what you know is true and repeat it to yourself. That way you won't get so confused with all these uncertainties."

"What do you mean?"

"Like those verses you wrote him from Philippians about how you thank God for him and how it's only right for you to feel that way because you hold him in your heart. He said he'd be your friend forever, remember? He promised you that."

"You're right. I need to remember a quote I used on my paper." Christy pulled out her essay and showed Katie. " 'My treasures are my friends.' "

"Yeah," Katie added, "and some friends are 'peculiar treasures.' I'd say Todd falls into the 'peculiar treasure' category."

The bell interrupted their pondering. Christy shoved her paper back in her notebook and said with a sigh, "I hope you're right, Katie."

"Of course I'm right. You know I'm right. Well, at least most of the time."

Christy smiled. "See you after school. I'm off to Spanish."

"My favorite subject lately," Katie said with her comical glint. "Don't forget to call your mom and see if you can take me home."

The remainder of the day went quickly, and Christy met Katie at her car. "My mom said it was fine for me to take you home. Is it okay if we stop at the post office first?"

"You're the driver," Katie said, dropping her books on the floor of the car. "How do you manage to keep your car so clean?"

"Mom's orders. She has a thing about dirty cars."

"I guess it doesn't hurt that your brother isn't old enough to borrow your car yet," Katie said.

When they were in front of the post office, Christy parked the car and asked Katie if she wanted to come in.

"Are you kidding? You've got my curiosity up on what this mysterious package is. Do you have the claim slip?"

"Right here," Christy said, pulling it out of her purse.

Four people were in line ahead of them, and soon five more people filed in behind them. When Christy reached the window, she handed the clerk the slip of paper and said, "I have a package with postage due. Here's the fifty-seven cents that are due on it."

"Just a moment," the clerk said and took off for the back with the slip in his hand. He returned right away with his hand behind his back and a funny grin on his face.

"Are you Christy Miller?" he asked.

"Yes."

"Do you know anyone named Phil?"

"Phil?" Christy turned to Katie to see if she recognized the name. "No, I don't think so."

"Just wondering," the clerk said. "Here you go." He

plopped a big, egg-shaped, greenish object on the counter. Her address was written on one side in thick black letters. "It's all yours."

"What's that?" Katie asked. "Some kind of overgrown kiwi?"

"No, it's a coconut," Christy said. "That's what they look like when they fall off the trees in Hawaii."

As soon as she said "Hawaii," her eyes grew big. She and Katie locked gazes, their mouths dropping open in unison. The girls quickly moved to the side wall, out of the way of the gawking customers.

"Turn it over, turn it over!" Katie urged. "What's written on the other side?"

Her heart pounding, Christy obediently turned over the coconut and spotted some more black letters. Aloud she read, " 'Phil. 1:7.' What does that mean?"

"Philippians!" Katie practically screamed. "Phil is short for Philippians. Don't you get it? He's sending your message back to you. I can't believe this! This is so incredible! What are those other words? They're kind of smeared. Can you read them?"

Christy held the coconut in the light, with Katie's face right beside hers. "I think it says, 'I . . . hold . . . you . . . in . . . my . . . heart . . . too.' "

"Ayhhhhhhhhhhh!" Both girls screamed and grabbed each other by the shoulders. Suddenly aware of their curious audience, Katie pushed Christy out of the post office and into the parking lot.

"What did I tell you? What did I tell you?" Katie said,

starting in a whisper and getting louder. "This is such a Todd-thing! Who else would ever think of mailing you a coconut? And sending back your message in Bible-verse code! This is so incredible!"

Christy looked at her coconut and then at her enthusiastic friend. Her vision turned blurry. She didn't know if the tears were from laughing or crying, because at this moment she wasn't sure which she was doing.

"Now, that," Katie said with a complete air of confidence, "is what I was talking about. You hold in your hand evidence that Todd is always going to be your true friend."

"He *is* my true friend, Katie," Christy said, blinking back the tears and hugging the coconut close to her heart. With her other arm she hugged Katie. "And you're my true friend too."

Don't Miss Christy's Other Adventures

Summer Promise *(Book 1)*—Christy spends the summer in Newport Beach with her wealthy aunt and uncle. Ultimately she has to decide if she will do whatever is necessary to force her summer to give her all it initially promised.

A Whisper and a Wish *(Book 2)*—Christy's family moves to southern California, and the most gorgeous guy in her new school gives her lots of attention. But disappointments are attached to every dream come true.

Yours Forever *(Book 3)*—Christmas break seems like the ultimate vacation, with a romantic picnic on the beach and a New Year's kiss. But Christy's relationships begin to fray as she tries her hand at some manipulations.

Surprise Endings *(Book 4)*—Cheerleader tryouts, and two dates for the prom set Christy's head to spinning with all the possibilities. But complications set in, especially when her parents object to so much socializing.

Island Dreamer *(Book 5)*—A surprise trip to Hawaii with her best friend and the guy of her dreams should have been a touch of paradise for Christy. But instead the trip is tinged with jealousy and flirty maneuvers.

A Heart Full of Hope *(Book 6)*—Christy's junior year begins with her going steady with a romantic, handsome guy. But then Christy is placed on restriction and her job interferes with her dating life.

To collect all the books in the Christy Miller Series, visit your local bookstore or contact Focus on the Family, Colorado Springs, CO 80995.